THE NORTH STAR INN

STACEY RAE

Sugarhouse Press, LLC

stacey@authorstaceyrae.com

CHAPTER ONE

Alice closed the front door behind her and exhaled. She hadn't realized she was even holding her breath. The early evening light streamed through the floor-to-ceiling windows of the sitting room she'd had installed so everyone could watch the sunset, even on the coldest days of the winter, and she was not disappointed with that investment.

The North Star Inn was ready. Guests would arrive in two days, and tomorrow was the launch party. The only thing missing was Peter North, Alice's husband of twenty-five years. The love of her life, her high school sweetheart, and her guiding light—her North Star.

The phone in Alice's back pocket rang, and she considered ignoring it. All she wanted was to relish her accomplishments of the last six months. She'd purchased this property almost as soon as Peter's life insurance money had hit her bank account, against the advice of her sisters, her daughters, her parents, and her friends.

"Don't rush into anything," her mother had told her.

"Take your time to get used to this change," her dad had said.

"You could travel anywhere, Mom. Weren't you and Dad just starting to talk about that?" Nora asked her. Alice and Peter's younger daughter had developed the travel bug during a college study abroad semester, and she was right; all of Nora's stories of adventure had gotten Alice and Peter talking. But that was Before. Before everything.

"Buy that boat you and Dad always wanted," Viv, Nora's older sister, advised her. It was true they'd spent years dreaming about a boat to take out on Lake Champlain in their retirement. But she didn't want to do that alone.

"Who needs a man at your age? Spend the money on yourself," her sister, Celia, had said. That stung, their fifteen-year age gap often causing a rift between them, but Alice took it with a grain of salt. She knew that Celia and Mitch had weathered some storms in their marriage over the years but had always prevailed, seeming to grow closer through every challenge.

"Save your money for retirement," her sister, Brooke said, always the planner. As an event planner, that shouldn't have surprised Alice, but she didn't heed her sister's advice.

Alice had gone ahead anyway and bought the neglected inn. The building had sat empty for years, and Alice knew it would take months to turn it into something she was happy with. And it had. Time, money, and plenty of sweat. Her dad helped, and Alice was thankful. He was the only reason it was ready now rather than a year from now. He hadn't let any of the construction team make excuses or get behind on the tight schedule.

Alice had been able to reconnect with her dad through the rebuilding process, and she'd learned enough about plumbing and electricity that she could now manage an emergency well-enough until a professional was available. She knew this skill would come in handy when she had an inn full of guests and needed a quick fix.

Her phone rang again and Alice relented. She reached into her back pocket and looked at the screen. Viv.

"Hi, Viv," she said.

"Hi, Mom. Are you at the Inn?" Viv asked. Alice could tell her daughter was distracted.

Alice walked to the tall windows and watched the sun glisten on the water of Lake Champlain and on the tarps covering one last surprise for tomorrow's event. The west lawn held half a dozen sculptures created by her lifelong friend, Marci Jewell.

Alice didn't want the North Star Inn to be set apart from the town, only attracting tourists. She wanted it to be part of the town, a place where locals as well as visitors could enjoy. And Marci's work was incredible. Alice was attracted to the contrast of the sharp metal sculptures with the softness of the lake behind them. She was excited to see the town's reaction tomorrow at the launch party.

"I am," she told her daughter, anticipating the excitement of the crowd at tomorrow's unveiling. The view out of these windows would be transformed. "It's all done. I got the last permit this afternoon, and good thing, too. Guests arrive on Friday. I don't know what I would have done if we hadn't pulled this off. Cancel my first weekend? What a disaster that would be. We already missed Memorial Day Weekend. I'm going to need guests all summer if this is going to turn a profit." She was rambling. It was the only way to keep the tears from coming. All she wanted was to share this day with Peter.

"Are you okay?"

Viv was almost too empathetic for her own good. As a

middle school teacher, that came in handy. But it also meant that Alice could almost never hide her emotions from her daughter.

Alice nodded. Of course, Viv couldn't see that. "I am." And she was.

"I'm coming over," Viv said.

"You don't have to do that. Don't you still have work tomorrow? And it's almost the end of the school year. You must be swamped with end-of-year grading." If Alice couldn't have Peter here to share in her joy, she wanted to be alone. Just for tonight. The North Star Inn was hers and she wasn't ready to share it yet.

"I can make time for you, Mom," Viv reassured her.

Alice smiled. Her relationship with her daughter had only strengthened as she'd gotten older. Middle school, of course, had been a challenging stretch, but what parent didn't struggle with that age? Alice thought that Viv's rebellious stretch was part of why she was such a great middle school teacher now. She could connect in a way that not all adults could with struggling and emotional preteens.

"I know you would, Viv. But really, I'm fine. I want to enjoy tonight, and I'll see you tomorrow evening at the launch party, right?"

"Wouldn't miss it for anything," Viv promised.

There was a pause, where Alice just appreciated her daughter's concern, before Viv said, "I'll see you tomorrow then. Love you, Mom."

"Love you, too."

Alice put the phone back in her pocket and took a last look at the lake before turning and walking to the dining room. This was her pride and joy. She'd had the same floor-to-ceiling windows installed on the east-facing side of the inn as well. This way, her guests would enjoy the sunrise while she served them breakfast.

There were four tables—one for each of the bedrooms named after seasonal constellations that Alice and Peter had made a tradition of finding—but she had a couple extras hidden away in case of events or extra guests coming by. The tables were hand-crafted in Vermont from maple trees on her old property. They had been in danger of coming down in a big windstorm anyway, so she'd had them harvested before she sold the place.

The tables were bare, and Alice intended to keep them that way. No tablecloths to hide the unique wood grains. The plates and bowls she intended to use were all hand-made by a local potter. And the placemats she'd recently purchased were woven by an old friend. Alice had spared no expense at pampering her guests while using the local markets.

The North Star Inn sat on a peninsula jutting into Lake Champlain, so there was no lack of stunning views. She'd made sure to allow her guests to enjoy the east, south, or west views from nearly any room in the inn. With parking on the north side, that had been easy to do.

Off of the dining room was Alice's second-favorite room —the kitchen. She'd loved cooking all her life, and cooking for one scared her. Cooking for others kept her going.

When Peter was diagnosed with an incurable brain tumor a year ago, today, Alice had spent the entire night baking. Peter stayed up with her, neither of them willing to spend a minute apart.

Peter's fainting, and then seizures, had sent them to the hospital, where they'd finally been given an answer: an incurable and inoperable glioblastoma. He'd been given four months to live but had eked out six. Alice was thankful for those extra two months with the love of her life, but it had all still gone too fast.

Alice and Peter hadn't eaten a thing from her marathon in the kitchen the night of Peter's diagnosis, instead giving it all away to her sisters, their daughters, friends, and parents when they'd broken the news. While the treats didn't keep the tears and heartbreak away, it at least gave them something to nibble on as they all imagined a future without Peter.

Cooking and baking were her therapy throughout it all, and had continued after he passed. If she and Peter hadn't found the North Star Inn at the right time, she would have opened a bakery. She felt lucky that they'd had the foresight to come up with a plan for After. While everyone thought Alice bought this building without a thought or a plan, she and Peter had been scheming since his diagnosis.

Alice had spent much of her life as a stay-at-home parent. She didn't have a recent work history that would get her a job, and she didn't want to spend the rest of her life sitting around living off Peter's life insurance. There was nothing in the world that she would have traded that time with her young daughters for, but she was now facing an uncertain future. Thankfully, the inn had been on the market for some time and the owners were desperate to sell. Peter helped make plans to turn it into what it was today.

He was her North Star throughout it all. And continued to be, even now.

This new kitchen was nearly identical to the one she'd shared with Peter in their house. Granite countertops, an island with a gas stove, a deep sink for all the dishes she'd have, huge windows with plants hanging in front of them, and the biggest difference—an extra-large fridge. If she was going to be cooking for a crowd most mornings, she wanted to make sure she had plenty of space for the best ingredients.

A lone envelope caught her attention on the counter. "Where did that come from?" Alice asked an empty room. She picked it up and her heart skipped a beat. Peter's handwriting was nearly illegible, but distinct.

Butterflies came to life in her stomach as Alice turned the plain envelope over in her hand. Someone had put it there. Someone had schemed with Peter to get it there.

Alice considered putting it back, not ready to read Peter's words, but she couldn't stop herself. He couldn't be here in person, but his spirit lived on. She slid a finger under the seal and peeled it open to read through her tears:

Alice –

You did it. The North Star Inn is ready for guests. I know you wish I was there to enjoy it with you, but this is all yours. You did this.

You are incredibly strong, smart, caring, and creative. Don't ever forget that. Your guests will be lucky to have you for their getaways.

Our daughters have been lucky to have you as their mother, and I was lucky to have you as my wife. Don't live in the past, wishing for what could have been. This is what is and there is no changing that. Look only to the future and find joy in each moment.

I love you,

Peter

Alice pulled a stool from the island to her and sat. She could barely see anymore. Peter's words cut straight to her heart. She knew he was right. It would be difficult to move past the love they shared; she would hold it close forever. She wouldn't move past it; that love would drive her forward.

The tears finally stopped and Alice took a deep breath. Mourning her loss would do her no good. She'd been lucky to be Peter's wife, but sadly that chapter was over.

Alice turned on the stove and put water on to boil. Tea would help settle her nerves.

While she waited, she made sure she had everything ready for tomorrow's launch party. She hadn't done the catering, though she'd floated the idea. She'd let her sister, Brooke, do the planning since the party grew bigger than Alice had expected. Brooke hired a caterer. Alice had to admit that it was a good thing. But the fridge was still stocked with plenty of drinks, just in case. Just in case of what, Alice wasn't sure. But it made her more confident that nothing could go wrong. At least no one would go thirsty.

The teapot whistled and Alice poured the boiling water over a peppermint tea bag in one of her favorite mugs—a painting Nora had done when she was just four years old. Peter had surprised Alice one Mother's Day decades ago by having their girls' artwork printed on mugs, to live forever in their kitchen. Alice used them daily, holding them close, and remembering what it was like to have her family all under one roof.

Alice took her tea to the sitting room and looked west once again. She thought back to Before. Before Peter's death. Before Peter's diagnosis. Before his illness's first signs. It was a dangerous path to walk down in her mind, but it was one she couldn't avoid.

"We should visit Europe," he'd told her not long before his first fainting episode. "Wouldn't it be incredible to see their history? It's nothing like here. It goes back centuries."

Alice knew he was right. But she'd hardly ever left the country. Shouldn't they start with exploring more of Canada? It was so close. She had no excuse anymore not to renew her passport and explore the world. They had the funds. They had the time. And the girls were out of college and on their own. It was time for them to enjoy each other.

Not that they didn't already do that. But to enjoy each other fully.

"Okay. Europe. We'll start there," she'd said, thinking that would be enough.

"Start there?" he'd said, raising an eyebrow, a smile lighting up his face and making his deep brown eyes twinkle with excitement. "And then to Africa, South America, the world is just waiting to be seen!"

Peter's sense of adventure was higher than hers. Which explained where Nora got hers from.

"That's not quite what I meant," she'd said, laughing.

But looking back now, she would have gone anywhere with him. She would have followed him to the moon if he'd asked.

Alice was brought back to the present when the front door suddenly opened. She just wanted to be alone with her memories, but she suddenly had company.

CHAPTER TWO

Brooke saw the surprise change to disappointment on Alice's face and almost turned around. Alice didn't want her and Celia here, that was clear.

"Alice," Celia crowed, speed walking toward their older sister. "This place is stunning."

Brooke took her shoes off, wishing that Celia had done the same. Alice had obviously had the place professionally cleaned after all the work was done and adding work for her was the last thing Alice needed them to do. With less than two days until the first guests were coming, the North Star Inn was spotless.

Alice slowly stood. "Thanks, Celia. I didn't know you guys were coming over. I would have made dinner."

Brooke held up two paper bags. "We brought it to you. We figured you had enough going on to cook for us."

"Thanks," Alice said, but she still didn't look happy with having company. The smile that twitched at the corners of her lips did not even come close to reaching her eyes.

Celia's mouth hung open as she took in the transformation. The building had been in need of some love, but Alice had gone above and beyond.

"I can't believe how much this has changed," Celia said. "I haven't seen it for months, I guess."

Brooke had come over at least once a week, sometimes bringing her three kids who loved helping their Grandpa build things. Since Alice had wanted to use the space for more than just a getaway, Brooke had consulted on making it an event space as well. Only for small events, and mostly outside, but there were a few things she'd seen that Alice hadn't.

Like having the public sculpture garden on the west lawn instead of on the south lawn that led down to the water. Allowing the public only on the west lawn kept the southern space private for paying guests. Finding those details was what made Brooke an in-demand event planner.

"Thanks," Alice told Celia, who continued to the other side of the Inn to check it all out. "What are you guys doing here?" Alice asked Brooke, not unkindly, but not welcoming, either.

"Dinner." Brooke smiled and walked into the kitchen to set the bags on the counter. "And to cover some last-minute details for tomorrow. I have an updated guest list. The select board chair finally RSVP'd; Greg is coming. I can't believe it took him until this afternoon to let me know. I've worked with him before and he's always late. But the day before? Anyway, a couple other smaller names have been added. I thought you'd want to know. The total count is fifty-six."

Alice's jaw dropped. It was supposed to be a small affair. Intimate, Alice had told Brooke when she'd offered to help. For free, of course. Alice tried to pay her, but Brooke wouldn't hear of it.

"I know, I know. You didn't want more than twenty-five, and this is more than double. Don't worry. I'll be there the whole time to work the crowd for you." Brooke knew big events were the things of Alice's nightmares. That was why an inn was the perfect business for her. No more than four couples at a time.

Brooke still didn't see Alice's face settle into happiness.

"Is everything okay? Are you having second thoughts?" Brooke asked her older sister. With eleven years between them, they hadn't exactly grown closer in adulthood. Brooke always felt like she was a generation behind Alice and could never catch up. There were moments when she felt like she was closing a gap between them—like when Brooke became a mother—but they were fleeting.

Alice shook her head. "Of course not." Her eyes darted to the counter and Brooke followed her gaze.

Before Brooke had a chance to pick up the envelope with Alice's name scribbled on it, her sister snatched it and slid it into her pocket. "It's nothing. I'm excited and nervous."

"And you wish Peter was here," Brooke said. She could see it on Alice's face; disappointment that he wasn't here.

Alice nodded.

Brooke put a hand on Alice's arm but had no words of comfort. She would be devastated if Jared suddenly passed. Her life was completely different from Alice's—Brooke had worked from the moment she finished school compared to Alice's stay-at-home parenting. Brooke barely took time off to have each of her three kids. She couldn't sit still long enough. Or trust anyone with her business.

The only blessing that Brooke saw was that Alice's girls were in their twenties. It had to still be hard on them as individuals and as a family to lose Peter, but at least they weren't dependent on Alice anymore.

"Those tables..." Celia gushed as she walked into the kitchen and made herself at home. "Are they from the trees you had taken down?"

"Yup," Alice said, turning to the stove and letting Brooke's hand fall back to her side, useless. "You guys want tea? The water should still be hot."

Brooke reached into one of the paper bags and pulled out a bottle of Champagne. "No expense spared for our big sister," she said. "Save the tea for your guests. Tonight, we're celebrating."

The smallest smile flashed on Alice's face but it still didn't reach her eyes. Brooke knew that she and Celia had their work cut out for them if they were going to get Alice to enjoy tonight, her first night at the North Star Inn. Hard work didn't intimidate Brooke. She was up for this challenge, just like every other one she faced head-on.

"And Nepali food from your favorite restaurant. We just picked it up," Brooke added. "Plates?"

Alice brought out three, placing them in a pile on the counter.

"What's under the tarps on the lawn?" Celia asked as she filled her plate. Brooke and Alice exchanged a look, and a true smile finally lit up her sister's face.

"You'll find out tomorrow," Alice teased, one eyebrow raising. "Just like everyone else. I think only three people know—myself, Brooke, and the person who made them."

Celia's spoon paused, mid-air, as she filled her plate. "Brooke, what are they?" she tried. But Brooke just shook her head.

"It's been the best-kept secret around here and my lips

are sealed. Don't be late tomorrow or you'll miss the unveiling. Five o'clock, sharp."

"Come on, guys. I can keep a secret," Celia begged, filling her plate and leaving the counter.

Alice and Brooke laughed. "No, you can't. Not even for twenty-four hours!" Brooke teased. "Remember that time Joey threw a rock through the Websters' garage window?" Celia's face turned red. Of course she remembered. "He made you promise not to tell, and you blurted it out as soon as Mr. Webster came outside!"

"I was twelve-years-old!" Celia said through laughter. "I'm not twelve anymore. But fine, I'll find out tomorrow."

Celia returned to the sitting room, and Brooke and Alice filled their plates and joined her.

"So, I have the caterer scheduled to come at two tomorrow. And music starts at 3:30. Guests are coming at four, speeches at 4:30, and tarps come off at five. I'll introduce you, then the artist speaks, then the tarps come off." Brooke was in her element, making sure everything was organized. She did this all day at work, then with her family of five.

Alice nodded and chewed.

"Do you have your speech ready?" Brooke asked.

"Of course." Alice tapped her temple.

Butterflies took off in Brooke's stomach. "You... have it written down, right?"

Alice smiled. "I do."

Brooke sighed. "Phew. You had me worried."

Alice laughed. "You are such a planner," she teased.

"I know. But it's my job." Brooke took a bite and moved on.

"When are Mom and Dad arriving?" Celia asked.

Brooke answered before Alice could. She knew it was a sore spot for her, and she couldn't blame her. "They're not.

They got stuck in South Carolina so they're going to miss it."

"What? You're kidding! This is Alice's huge event and they're not even going to be here?"

Brooke agreed that they should have tried harder. They'd been on their way back from their winter in Florida —later than they usually drove back to Vermont since they'd arrived to Florida later with Dad's work on the Inn with Alice—and they'd ended up with RV trouble along the way. Now they were waiting for a part and staying with a friend. Brooke told them to book a flight and she'd pick them up and lend them a car. But they'd refused.

"They'll see it all when they get here," Alice assured them. "Dad did so much work on it that it won't be a big surprise." She sounded falsely confident.

"Have Nora and Viv seen it all finished yet?" Celia asked. Alice nodded. "Can I check out the rooms?" Alice nodded again and Celia brought her plate to the kitchen. "I'll be right back", she called.

"Now I can finally tell you the really exciting change I have—Marci agreed to change the sculpture garden quarterly to match the seasons. So this is just going to be the summer exhibit," Brooke whispered. She kept one eye on the view outside and one on the door leading to the stairs down to the bedrooms. No one was supposed to know this change until the fall when Marci unveiled new sculptures that she was still working on, specifically for the Inn's lawn.

Alice coughed, nearly choking. "That's amazing. But she doesn't have to do that. I thought this was going to be a permanent exhibit."

Brooke nodded. "That had been the plan, but then Marci had this vision and she's going for it. Keep it under wraps, though. If she's late on her pieces, she doesn't want to be held to a timeline she can't meet."

Alice laughed. "I understand that. I barely made this weekend's opening. Last permit came through just this afternoon. I was getting nervous I'd have to cancel!"

Brooke knew that would have been disastrous, at least in the short term. Everything would have had to be rescheduled. Nothing Brooke couldn't have dealt with—she could negotiate her way into and out of practically anything with anyone—but far from ideal at the last minute.

And not only that, but Alice had dumped pretty much all of her savings and inheritance into renovations and needed it to open for the summer when tourists were flocking to Vermont.

"Well, we don't have to worry about that now." Celia walked back in and Brooke leaned back in her chair. "What'd you think?" she asked, changing the subject back to the Inn's transformation.

"I love it," Celia said. "The screen porch looks so inviting and relaxing, and the bedrooms all have great views of the lake. It feels so private downstairs. You did a great job making everything bright and giving each room its own unique feel. I can guess which one is for honeymooners." She smiled and paused. "Peter would love it, too. He'd be proud."

Alice nodded. "He would be," she agreed, her eyes going distant. "He actually wrote me a note about it. Specifically for tonight when the Inn was ready to go." She turned to Brooke and pulled the envelope out of her pocket. "That's what you saw on the counter. Did either of you put it there?"

Brooke hadn't. She turned to her younger sister, but

Celia just looked confused. "How did he know about it?" she asked. "You bought it after he passed."

Alice smiled. "We made plans together before he died. He knew what I was going to do with his life insurance money."

Brooke's mouth fell open. "And you just let us all tell you not to do it?"

A laugh finally escaped from Alice, and Brooke knew her sister would be okay. Maybe not tonight, but eventually. Peter's love would carry her forward.

"Yup. I needed a piece of Peter for myself still."

Celia playfully hit Alice's arm. "I can't believe you."

"You can't believe her because she kept a secret all this time when you can't even keep one for a day," Brooke said, and all three sisters dissolved into laughter.

"We forgot the Champagne!" Celia finally managed through her continued giggles.

"How did we manage that?" Brooke returned to the kitchen and found three glasses. She brought the Champagne back out to the sitting room where she saw the colors in the sky grow more and more stunning. "What's the trick to opening this without making a mess? You don't need a flood before you even open."

Alice took the bottle and untwisted the metal cage on top of the cork. "Keep it at a forty-five-degree angle. Then the bubbles won't explode over my beautiful—and clean—floors." More laughter ensued before a loud pop made them all cheer.

"To Alice," Celia said when their three glasses were full.

"And Peter," Brooke added, catching Alice's eye. She could see the faintest hint of tears starting to swim over the blue of her eyes. Whatever kept the sisters apart, they were still family and that never ended.

Alice smiled and they all took a sip.

Brooke felt that she and Celia were turning a corner in their relationships with Alice as the evening continued. It wasn't often that Alice opened up to them, but with her best friend and confidant gone, she was becoming a new person; a different sister.

"Will Peter's parents be there tomorrow?" Celia asked.

Alice nodded. "I invited them to stay at the Inn after since I won't have guests but they'd already booked a room elsewhere. I thought it only fitting that they were the first guests."

"How are they doing?" Brooke asked.

Alice shrugged. "As well as can be expected. They lost their only son." The tears seemed to magically stay in Alice's eyes rather than spill down her cheeks. Brooke wasn't sure how she managed.

"And Nora and Viv?" Brooke added as gently as she could.

"The same. We're all managing. It's a new normal," Alice admitted. "One we have to get used to and make the best of. We had him for so long, the six months he's been gone feels like a single moment."

A moment of silence passed before Alice asked, "Is Jared bringing the kids tomorrow?"

"Just for a little while. Emma still has to get to bed reasonably early or we all suffer. We have a babysitter, though. He'll come back after he brings them home." Brooke's four-year-old was a fireball of energy and would love to stay all night, but she'd still get up early the next morning, overtired and overstimulated.

"And Mitch?" Alice asked, turning to Celia.

A long pause almost made Brooke blurt out the truth. It was time for Celia to come clean. "Just me," Celia said. "He's out of town."

"For work?"

Celia didn't answer, instead looking down at her hands clasped in her lap. Brooke knew that honesty was the only thing that would bring her and Celia closer to Alice, and she wanted that. For everyone. But this was apparently the one secret that her younger sister was able to keep.

CHAPTER THREE

Celia stashed her bike in her office and fluffed her short hair back out. Biking the six miles to Celia's Bookshelf was her favorite way to start the day, and helmet hair was part of that deal.

Her bookstore brought Celia more joy than anything—except maybe Mitch until four months ago. Looking through boxes of new or used books was better than Christmas. At least, better than Christmas since she found out Santa wasn't real. As the youngest kid, that had happened sooner than she wished.

Celia could admit now that her marriage wasn't perfect. They'd had their moments in the past that had been hard, but nothing compared to what was going on now—now that they'd been separated for four months, caused by something Celia couldn't even guess. Mitch hadn't explained it when he'd moved out.

No matter what, Celia wasn't ready to throw in the towel.

Celia was still kicking herself for not telling Alice the truth last night. She'd been given the perfect opportunity when Alice asked if Mitch was coming to the launch party tonight. No, he wouldn't be coming. But no, it wasn't because he was out of town for work like she'd let Alice believe.

He was out of town because he'd moved out.

Four months ago.

Asked for a divorce two months ago. And only Brooke knew.

"Why didn't you tell her?" Brooke had demanded as soon as they were in her car last night. Celia had practically pulled Brooke out of Alice's after the mood turned sour with the mere mention of Mitch.

"She doesn't need more on her plate right now," Celia said, unable to look at her sister.

"Doesn't need more—come *on*, Celia. She's our sister! So what if you think she still sees you as the baby of the family. Guess what—you're acting the part right now."

Celia knew Brooke was right. She was being stubborn. The only secret she could keep was that her marriage was faltering. No, it wasn't even doing that anymore. It was on life support and the plug was about to be pulled.

"Alice doesn't need to be distracted by my own problems when she's obviously still dealing with Peter's death and is now focused on opening the Inn," Celia defended.

Brooke started the car without a response. If Celia could have just kept her mouth shut, they would have driven in silence.

But she didn't keep her mouth shut. "And I'm still trying to get Mitch to go to counseling. Or at least talk to me. We can work this out."

Brooke shook her head. "You told me last week that you don't even know why you aren't signing the papers."

Celia took a deep breath. She wished she hadn't told

Brooke that anymore. It would be what drove Celia and Mitch apart; Celia's own questioning of their marriage.

"You want to know what I think?" Brooke asked. She didn't wait for Celia to tell her no, she didn't want to know. "I think you aren't telling Alice because you still hold a grudge from college. Alice didn't come to your college graduation because Viv was in the hospital. A thirteen-year-old child who needed her mother. And now you use whatever excuse you can find to get back at her. You don't think Alice ever makes time for you. You always thought it was a competition."

"That's not fair," Celia whispered. It was true though; she'd been mad for years that Alice couldn't let Peter stay with Viv in the hospital for just a couple hours so Alice could see Celia walk across the stage. But that was ancient history now. A lifetime ago.

"Well, if that's not it, what is it that makes you keep such a big secret from Alice? You know she'd do everything she can to help you."

"I don't want her help," Celia nearly shouted.

That was when the car went silent for the rest of the drive. Brooke had dropped her off and Celia slammed the car door without another word.

This morning, Celia had her regrets. Of course she should have told Alice. Of course Alice would help her. Knowing the truth would probably bring them closer together—closer than they'd ever been.

Celia had been a toddler when Alice went away to college. She'd idolized her all through grade school, only learning that she wasn't a goddess when she reached her teens. Rather than rebelling against her parents, Celia had pushed Alice away. Now, more than half her life later, they still hadn't reconciled.

The Keurig gurgled, giving Celia hope that she'd get through today. She could talk to Alice after her event. She'd stay and help clean up; make up for last night. Take the first step toward making up for the last twenty years.

Celia almost never let herself indulge in a second cup of coffee, sticking to one at home and drinking water at work. But after her night with Alice and Brooke, she'd barely slept and woken tired. She knew she'd pay for the extra caffeine tonight when she lay awake, mind racing, but she went ahead and made a second cup anyway. The coffee finished and she picked up her mug.

There was nothing to do but move forward. Forward with Alice. Forward with Mitch. Forward with her life.

The bells on the door jangled and Celia pushed all thoughts of her personal troubles out of her mind. She was at work and focused on her customers.

"Good morning," she said to a regular. "You finish your last book?"

"I did," Ian Meadows said with a smile. His eyes were always hidden by a ball cap but today he took it off, making him almost look like a stranger. "It was another hit. Jenna even picked it up and gave it a chance."

"And...?" Celia asked. She'd never met Ian's wife but knew her reading preferences. Ian's favored fantasy was not what she went for.

Ian shook his head. "I think she read three pages before she went back to her romance. I'll never understand it. She just wants happily ever afters."

"Don't we all, though?" Celia asked. She could sure use one.

"In life, sure. But I'll take witches and vampires any day in fiction. What do you have that's new?" he asked, picking up a title from the new release table.

Celia left her coffee on the counter without giving it a second thought. Now that there was work to do, she was focused and alert. "Your wife will love this new series, I think. You could start with just book one if you want to and I can put the others away on hold, just to be safe. And for you—" She turned a corner and indicated for Ian to follow. "I put this aside for you as soon as it came in. Original print. Mint condition. Totally transformed the genre. Not new, but if you haven't read it, you should."

Ian smiled. "When did you get it in?"

"Two weeks ago. I think it was a clean-out of a grandparent. I found it in the bottom of a box of kids' books. I thought of you right away."

"How much?" Ian asked, looking concerned as he turned the book over in his hands. Drool was practically falling from his mouth.

"I'll give you a deal. I don't think they knew what they had. They wanted the box rate, thinking it was just a bunch of kids' books. This alone is worth at least $250. I'll sell it to you for a hundred." Celia had felt guilty when she'd found this at the bottom of the box. But a sale was a sale and the sellers had wanted to be quick. They weren't concerned with each individual title. They just wanted to move on.

"I don't know."

"Eighty," Celia offered. "I really can't go any lower."

Ian got a faraway look in his eyes, maybe imaging the cover on a shelf in his living room. If she didn't have a business to run, Celia would have given it to him for free. He was such a regular customer—loyal almost to a fault. But with the way bookstores were closing everywhere, crippled by box store and online competition, Celia knew she couldn't pass up making at least a few dollars on this gem.

"Okay. I'll call it a Father's Day gift."

Celia sighed in relief. "I didn't know you had any kids."

"Not yet. But Jenna's due in October with our first." Ian glowed at the news.

"Congratulations! Do you know if it's a boy or a girl?"

"Girl. Don't ask for names, though. Our list is a mile long."

Celia laughed. She walked the long way back to the register through the used section and grabbed two of her favorite kids' books.

"These are a gift. If Jenna isn't happy with your Father's Day gift, give her these." Celia handed them to Ian and he smiled. In another life—one without Jenna or Mitch—she could see herself being happy with him. She was always happy when he walked into Celia's Bookshelf. She instantly berated herself for even thinking that when all she wanted was for Mitch to come home.

"Thanks, Celia. That means a lot."

She rang up his total and Ian winced. He handed over his card anyway. "Do you want them wrapped? The kids' books, I mean."

He hesitated but then shook his head. "I can manage that part. I think. I guess it'll be kind of like swaddling, right? Wrapping up books and wrapping up a baby?"

Celia laughed again. "I wouldn't know. But it sounds like you've been practicing. I'm sure you'll do just fine."

The most time Celia spent with a baby was when Brooke had Emma four years ago. By then, Noah and Tina were six and two and wild animals. Brooke would take them to a playground or the pool, and Celia wore Emma while the baby napped. She had never changed a diaper or dealt with a baby carrier alone. Brooke or Jared was always there to help her.

"Thanks again, Celia," Ian said as he picked up his

paper bag. "I'll see you in a month or so for my next book. Maybe before if Jenna loves this one."

Celia waved then picked up her coffee, taking a deep breath. It was still steaming hot.

The rest of the morning was slow, punctuated by a few customers who were more interested in browsing than finding anything specific. This gave Celia plenty of time to sort through more used books and reshelve anything left on tables. The children's section was the most prone to books being left around, but that only made Celia proud that she had created a place for kids to come and enjoy.

The quiet of the store also gave her time to think about Alice and Mitch, both subjects that she'd have liked to be distracted from.

The last four months brought out too many emotions for her. Mitch had asked for a break after Celia told him that she'd invested in new shelves for the used section of her bookstore. It had been on her list of needs for years, and she finally felt that she had the financial stability to take the leap. She replaced her outdated metal shelves with beautiful wood ones.

Sure, it had been expensive, but in her opinion it made a huge difference. Customers who may have skipped over the used section before were now drawn in by the warmer atmosphere.

But Mitch hadn't seen it that way. He'd thought it was frivolous.

"Couldn't you have found used shelves to sell used books on?" he'd said when she told him she'd finally bit the bullet and went through with the purchase.

Celia hadn't even responded. She was dumbstruck. His support had always been unwavering so she'd been completely caught off guard.

"Sorry, that wasn't a nice thing to say," he admitted almost immediately. "It just seems like maybe you could have talked to me first. I would have helped you find the best price."

"I have talked to you about this. For years," she said when she found her voice again. "I didn't know you wanted to help. You never offered."

"I didn't know you were getting serious about it."

Celia once again had nothing to say.

"Look. I think we should take a break," he'd dropped on her then. Out of nowhere. Celia hadn't seen it coming at all.

Though, looking back now, she should have seen the signs. Hindsight was so clear. Or maybe she was just looking for the signs now and making something of nothing. She couldn't tell.

Celia and Mitch had never combined their bank accounts when they married. It was easy to keep things separate. They each had their own businesses—Celia had Celia's Bookshelf and Mitch his landscaping—so it had made sense to keep everything separate. It had actually been Celia's idea.

They had a joint account, too. And they each contributed the same amount each month to cover their shared expenses. But anything that was "extra" or business-related came out of their separate accounts.

And Celia's was dwindling. Especially after buying the new shelves.

"Is this about the shelves?" Celia asked Mitch the next morning when he was packing a suitcase.

He shook his head. "Of course not."

"Have you been planning to ask for a break? Is it about money?" she asked. After he'd told her he wanted to take a break, she'd gone to their bedroom and hadn't seen him until the next morning. This was her only chance, she felt, to ask him where this was coming from.

"It's not about money," he told her, zipping the suitcase closed.

"But you've been thinking about a break for a while, then." She didn't ask this time.

Mitch still didn't answer or look at her. "I'm going to stay at Stuart's for a while."

Celia simply nodded. She'd never been close with his brother. Staying there would mean Celia probably wouldn't show up unannounced.

Mitch had walked out.

Just like that.

In the last four months, Brooke was the only person she'd told the whole truth to. It had been easy to keep it quiet from her parents—especially when they'd left for Florida. She rarely saw Alice. And when she did, they mostly just talked about the Inn and Peter and how Alice was doing. There hadn't been an obvious time to tell Alice what was going on.

Not until last night.

The divorce request had come two months later. Celia was shocked. Again.

Mitch had refused to come back home. He'd refused to try counseling. He'd refused to meet for coffee. Celia still didn't know why he suddenly wanted a divorce.

Because she wanted to try to have a baby? She hadn't brought that up in a year.

Because he wanted to move somewhere warmer? They both had established businesses here. He claimed it'd be easier to have a landscaping business somewhere with a shorter winter, and he was probably right. But moving would mean starting from scratch.

Because he just wanted to live a bachelor lifestyle again? Was it nothing but a midlife crisis a little early? Thirty-four was hardly midlife.

Mitch had even refused to meet her with his lawyer. He had given her everything in the divorce papers. He wasn't even asking for part of her business income or retirement savings. She got the condo. The joint bank account. Even alimony, though she wasn't sure why. She worked. She had a profitable business. Did he really want out that badly?

The only silver lining she saw in all of this mess was that there were no kids. Celia couldn't imagine the emotional toll this would take on a young child. She knew plenty of kids who made it through, at least appearing to be fine. And in the long term, they probably were.

Maybe never having kids with Mitch was a blessing in disguise.

The bells on the door jangled and Celia turned to see Cori enter. "Sorry I'm late," the teen said, looking sheepish. "Debate team ran late."

"No problem. I hadn't even noticed the time," Celia told her. Cori was always conscientious about being on time, and if she was late it was always for a good reason. Celia couldn't fault the high school senior for investing her time in worthwhile pursuits. "I thought that was done for the year, though."

"Today was the last day. There's only one week of school left. This was the farewell."

"And then graduation and college," Celia said. "I'm going to miss you in the fall."

Cori beamed at the praise. "I'll just be at UVM. I could come work on weekends." She hung her bag behind the counter and looked through the box of books for reshelving.

"I haven't filled your position yet. Haven't even started

looking," Celia promised. "I'd be happy to keep you on for the weekends, but I don't want you to stretch yourself too thin, either."

Cori picked up the box. "I guess we'll cross that bridge when the time comes. I'll get this done and then start on the boxes of new books?"

"Perfect. Thanks, Cori. You're still good closing today, right?" She hardly ever asked her to take on that added responsibility.

"Of course," Cori called over her shoulder.

Celia checked the time and saw that she had half an hour if she was going to make it to Alice's event on time. She had to admit that she was curious to see what was under the tarps. There were no customers at the moment, so Celia closed out her work on the computer—researching some new early chapter books for elementary age kids—and headed to the bathroom.

When she made it back to the front counter, Cori was there too. "I'll see you tomorrow afternoon. If there's an emergency, call. I can always come back."

"An emergency? Like I find a bookworm in one of the new books?" Cori teased.

Celia laughed and grabbed her bike from her office. She regretted riding it now. When she'd left this morning, all she'd been thinking about was her frustration with Mitch and Alice and herself. She'd forgotten that she'd have to ride home in the dark tonight.

Out front, Celia put everything into her saddlebags and was just about to ride away when her cell phone rang. She almost didn't answer it, knowing it could make her late if she did. But like so many other people, she was too tied to technology to ignore it.

She pulled it out of her pocket while she straddled her bike and saw Mitch's name.

Maybe he was calling to say he was coming home. This had all been a mistake.

Celia could dream, right?

She knew that was likely far from the truth but she answered with hope in her heart anyway.

"Hi," she said.

"Celia." There was a moment of silence, like he was waiting for her to make this conversation easy for him. She had plenty to say, but didn't even know where to start. This was the first time he'd reached out in four months. She was speechless. "I talked to my lawyer again. Why won't you sign the divorce papers, Celia?"

Celia took a deep breath before answering. "Can't we at least try to make this work?" She was nearly begging.

A sigh came through the phone and she winced. "Celia, I just don't know—"

"Can't we go to counseling? It can help, Mitch. We made a promise to each other. Doesn't that mean anything to you?"

"Celia, sign the papers." His words didn't match his tone. There was no hardness in his voice. Did he not want the divorce?

Celia's blood boiled. She wanted to shout at him. But it wouldn't work. She hung up the phone and pedaled off, unsure how to fix something when she didn't know how it broke.

CHAPTER FOUR

Alice took one last look at the lake and turned around. This was it. Brooke would arrive any minute, followed by the caterer, the band, Marci, and guests. The North Star Inn was open for business.

She walked from the south lawn toward the sculpture garden to the west of the Inn and saw someone walking among the towering tarps. But it wasn't Brooke.

"Nora," Alice called, waving to her younger daughter. "You're early."

"I know," Nora said. "It was a slow day so I came over in case you needed any last-minute help."

Nora worked in the study abroad office at UVM, where she graduated from just over a year ago. She was trying her best to travel for work but hadn't been able to get her foot in the door. Yet. Alice knew these things took time, but Nora thought it should have all fallen into place by now.

"I imagine there's not a whole lot going on between semesters," Alice agreed.

Nora nodded. "But we'll start getting international students for the summer semester soon. And I'm helping with their orientation. Fingers crossed that I'll get to move to the Office of International Education. Way more travel opportunities then."

If that was Nora's goal, then Alice hoped she would get transferred there, too.

"This looks kind of creepy," Nora said, gesturing toward the covered sculptures. "Like a ghost graveyard or something."

Alice laughed. She checked the time on her watch and said, "Give it three hours and it will have a totally different feel. Brooke and the caterer should be here any minute." She turned and checked the driveway but there was no movement. There was still plenty of time, she told herself. Alice had thought that two o'clock was early for a four o'clock start, but Brooke was boss.

"Did you find Dad's card last night?" Nora asked, bringing Alice's attention back to the Inn.

She didn't answer right away, not having guessed that Nora had anything to do with placing Peter's letter on the kitchen counter. "That was you?" she asked once she'd figured out what her daughter was talking about.

Nora nodded. "He gave it to me nine days before he died. He couldn't tell me when I was supposed to give it to you. I had to ask a million questions to figure out what was going on." Nora's gaze headed out over Lake Champlain and Alice let her have a moment with her memory.

Peter had lost the ability to talk weeks before he passed away. But he'd still been cognitively sharp. He could blink once for yes, twice for no to tell them what he needed. Alice had struggled to keep the tears at bay any time she couldn't guess his needs within a couple questions. But Nora had been the one to stay strongest.

Viv, with her extra empathy, had broken down nearly

every time she'd seen her father. Understandably so. But that didn't help anyone.

Nora had spent hours reading to Peter, Alice keeping busy in another room so she was nearby to help if needed. And also to hear the joy in Nora's voice as she related tales of her travels when they took a break from the day's book. They'd all heard her stories by then, but Alice loved listening to them a second, third, and fourth time.

"I must have asked him fifty questions before I guessed that it was a letter for the Inn's opening." Nora chuckled. "He looked like he had sand in his eyes he was blinking twice for no so many times." This time Alice chuckled, too.

"Thank you," Alice whispered, putting her hand on Nora's arm. "Thank you for helping him share his final words with me."

"Who says those were his final words?" Nora lifted an eyebrow, an expression so much like Peter's that it jolted Alice's heart.

Alice smiled. "I can wait to find out."

"I'm kidding. I don't have anything else from him."

Alice nodded. "It was just what I needed last night."

She couldn't convey to her daughter just how much Peter's words had meant to her in the moment. Alice felt that she was moving on without Peter, which, of course she was. She was still alive.

But now she knew that she was doing so with his full blessing. And she had Nora to thank for bringing that comfort at such a hard time.

"Dad always knew exactly what we needed to hear, when we needed to hear it," Nora said.

Alice didn't have time to respond before she heard tires on the gravel driveway. She turned to find Brooke's car arriving, followed by an Otto's Catering Services van.

"This is it, then," Alice told Nora. "You can head inside if you want to check things out. Oh—you probably did that when you stuck the card in there."

Nora smiled sheepishly. "I did. I hope that's okay."

"Of course it is. You'll always have a place in my home." She hugged Nora, and then they walked together to the driveway.

"Sorry we're late," Brooke said as she closed her driver's door. "I asked Otto to come at 2:30 instead. You were right, two was kind of early. I'm used to much bigger events."

One man—Alice assumed he was Otto—and two young women exited the van and got straight to work with barely a wave of greeting.

"I would have loved a heads-up," Alice told Brooke. "I was starting to get worried."

"Worried? About an event I organized? Leave that to me," Brooke teased. Then she turned and brought Otto down to the west lawn to show him exactly where everything went.

"I think I will go inside for a minute," Nora said. "But really, if you need help with anything, I'm here for that."

"Thank you," Alice said, then walked to the west lawn to check on plans.

Alice walked between the covered sculptures one more time, again imaging what the guests would think. Had she made the right choice by asking Marci to install a sculpture garden here? Was she trying to do too much? Would guests at the Inn feel too much town encroachment when they were trying to have a quiet weekend away?

What would Peter think of the final product? she wondered.

Alice would never know, and that pulled at her heartstrings in an unexpected moment of crushing sadness.

"Alice," Brooke called. "This will come off first, right?" She was at the westward-most sculpture, Alice's favorite.

"No. Last. Let's start closest to the Inn and work our way west."

Brooke didn't answer for a moment. Alice had changed plans at the last minute. But she wanted to save the best for last.

"Okay... okay. That'll work. Okay." Alice had actually flustered Brooke. She didn't think it was possible.

Brooke nodded as she walked back to Alice, still digesting the change. When she reached Alice, she stopped.

"Are you and Celia okay?" Brooke asked her older sister.

Alice was taken aback by the question. She'd been wondering the exact same thing since well before last night. Alice had felt their relationship growing more and more strained since she'd married Peter. She'd told herself it was just their age difference, always trying to bridge their age gap.

But last night felt different. Last night felt like Celia was hiding something from Alice. Something about Mitch.

"I'm not really sure," Alice said slowly. "Why do you ask?"

Brooke seemed to consider her answer before saying, "Because Mitch asked for a divorce two months ago and I got the feeling she hasn't told you."

Alice's mouth fell open. She was right. Celia was keeping something from her about Mitch. But why? Alice had been nothing but supportive of her youngest sister her entire life. She'd always felt that she had to be the bigger person when Celia got in one of her moods and lashed out at her. She was fifteen years older, after all. She had a responsibility to be a role model to both of her sisters, but Celia had always made that hard.

"I had no idea," Alice said.

Brooke turned toward the water. "I didn't think you did. I don't think Mom and Dad know either." She suddenly turned back to Alice. "You won't say anything to her, will you?"

"Of course not." This hadn't been Brooke's news to share, but Alice was sure that she was just looking out for their sister. If she was in trouble—emotionally, in this case—they would all drop everything to help her.

If she wanted their help.

"What happened with them?" Alice asked. Now that she'd scratched the surface on what was up with Celia, she had to dig deeper.

Brooke shook her head. "I'm not really sure. I don't think Celia even knows. But Mitch suddenly asked for a break and moved out four months ago—"

"Four months?" Alice nearly shouted.

Brooke nodded. "He's been staying with Stuart, apparently. Celia hasn't seen him since. He doesn't call. He refuses to go to counseling."

Alice was stunned. "She's hiding it well," she admitted.

Brooke chuckled and nodded. "Yeah. She's always been good at doing that. For all the secrets she can't keep, she doesn't show her feelings."

"Maybe tonight we'll be able to get her to open up about it. After the party's over. You're staying, right?" Alice asked.

"For a little while at least. I have another bottle of Champagne. And Jared's coming back, too."

"Right."

"There's Marci," Brooke said, pointing toward the sculpture garden. "I'll go tell her about the change in the order of revealing the sculptures. And that means the band will be here soon, too." She started walking back toward the west lawn, Alice falling behind to digest the news about Celia and Mitch.

Alice watched Brooke manage everything as it happened—Marci, the band, Greg's arrival, even Peter's parents. She was made for this job.

As guests began to arrive in greater numbers, Alice was reminded that she was not made for this kind of event. She'd always had Peter to help her through parties in the past. He was the one who started small talk with acquaintances and showed her how to mingle with anyone. Now she had to use the memory of him to guide her through her own launch party.

"Alice, this is incredible," Peter's mother, June, told her. The band had started and Alice led Mr. and Mrs. North away from their small stage so they could talk more comfortably.

"A sight to behold," his father, Robert, agreed.

"Thank you," Alice said, hugging them each in turn. "I just wish Peter was here to share it."

June placed a hand on Alice's arm. "We all wish that, dear. A part of me knows he is here. Somehow."

Alice was at a loss for words. She'd struggled with talking about Peter to his own parents ever since his death. Not that she'd had ample opportunity. There had been the memorial, of course. And they'd chatted on the phone a few times. But this was the first time since Peter passed away that they were all together.

"I hope you enjoy tonight. Peter helped plan everything," Alice told them. "Before he passed. We made these plans together."

"I had no idea," June said, looking surprised.

Alice smiled. "I know. We didn't tell anyone. I held him close those last months."

"We all did," June agreed.

"I know he'd be proud," Robert said.

Alice nodded, catching the pain in Robert's eyes. "I know."

Brooke sidled up to her and whispered, "I'm about to introduce you. You ready?"

"Excuse me," Alice said to Peter's parents, and she walked with Brooke toward the microphone.

"You ready?" Brooke asked again.

Alice took a deep breath and nodded. Brooke left her to the side of the band to take center stage. Alice barely heard a word she said, but when the crowd began clapping and Brooke turned toward her, she knew it was her turn to speak.

She walked toward Brooke, took the microphone, and said the words she'd practiced over and over in her mind.

"Thank you for coming this afternoon to welcome the North Star Inn to town. I can't think of anywhere else I'd like to be than right here, on the shores of Lake Champlain, to welcome guests to enjoy our beautiful slice of heaven."

She paused for more clapping, then continued. "Many of you know that the love of my life, Peter North, passed away six months ago."

Alice scanned the crowd and found many of the faces that meant the most to her—Nora and Viv stood together, June and Robert held hands, and Jared had three kids hanging off of him, Alice's nieces and nephew. She looked for more faces and saw her good friends Helen and Irene, and even Irene's brother, Will.

"What many of you don't know is that Peter helped plan the North Star Inn before he passed away. It was the final labor of love that we shared."

A few murmurs rippled through the crowd and Alice looked for the one face she hadn't found yet—Celia's.

"I wouldn't be standing here without his love and support. Now I ask that you love and support what we created for all to enjoy."

There was more applause, and Brooke took the microphone from her. Alice listened as she introduced Marci, sounds of surprise and excitement coming from those around her.

Alice soon found herself sandwiched between Nora and Viv. "Good job, Mom," Nora whispered, hugging her.

"Dad helped?" Viv asked, stunned. "I had no idea." Alice saw a sly smile spread across Nora's face. "You knew?" Viv asked her sister, disbelief making her jaw drop.

Nora nodded.

"And you didn't tell me? Since when do we keep secrets from each other?" Viv asked, sounding slightly hurt. Alice loved that her daughters were still such good friends in adulthood.

"He made me promise," Nora whispered.

Alice shushed her daughters just before the first tarp was removed.

Alice had hand-selected the sculptures she wanted in the sculpture garden. They were all stunning, but Alice couldn't wait for the sixth one to be revealed.

This first one was abstract, very angular. She liked the hardness of it. The severity of the angles. Especially with the water in the background.

Alice watched as each tarp was removed, getting the crowd more and more excited. When the last tarp finally came off, Alice breathed a sigh of relief. It was all here now. She was ready.

The twelve stars of the sculpture were perfect for the

North Star Inn. They were arranged in such a way that it looked like the sculpture itself was defying gravity. Each star was bigger than the last as they climbed up to the highest one, curving around in an arc.

Marci had told her the secret to how she'd been able to balance them. "The bottom ones are solid metal, giving the base plenty of weight. But the top ones are hollow. They're actually really light. It took me forever to get the metal thin enough so the sculpture wouldn't topple over."

They'd still pounded the support pole six feet into the ground to make sure. The last thing anyone needed was for a sculpture to crash over. They'd done the digging by hand in the dark of night so no one would know what was going on. It had taken several nights of Alice, Brooke, and Marci working together to get the hole big enough for their team to install it.

Their work was totally worth it. The crowd gazed in amazement, and Alice saw joy and triumph written across Marci's face.

Brooke took center stage again, congratulating Marci on her work and installation to the permanent sculpture garden at the North Star Inn. Alice remembered that it was still a secret that they would change the sculptures seasonally.

Greg took the microphone from Brooke to say his piece. He spoke of community involvement and the joy of creating a space for everyone to enjoy—residents and visitors alike. He made sure not to take credit for anything, but congratulated Alice and Marci on their hard work to make everything happen so quickly.

When he finished, Alice was bombarded with guests coming up to her to share their admiration of what she and Peter had created. Many expressed happiness at finally having the Inn renovated. The previous owner had been unable to afford to keep it up and it had fallen into disrepair, creating an eyesore along the shore.

"It was ingenious to add the sculptures," Irene told her, her older brother Will looking just as impressed. "I love the one with stars. Perfect for the North Star Inn."

Alice nodded in agreement.

"It almost looks like it's held up by magic," Will added. Alice smiled at the thought. Maybe the Inn did hold a little bit of magic. She couldn't wait to find out.

Alice spent the rest of the event slightly distracted. She couldn't stop looking for Celia. She thought she spotted her multiple times, but was always disappointed.

Now that Alice knew what was going on with her and Mitch, her heart softened for her youngest sister. She couldn't begrudge Celia for being cold toward her when she had her own struggles. She only wished that her sister would tell her so she could offer support.

No matter how hard Alice tried, she couldn't find Celia. By the time the final guest left, she hadn't seen her sister at all.

Alice wondered if Celia was okay. And if her and Celia's relationship had turned a corner for the worse.

CHAPTER FIVE

"You should have seen June and Robert's faces when the final tarp came off," Brooke gushed to Alice as they relaxed into chairs in the sitting room. She was beyond thrilled with how the launch party had turned out. Peter's parents' faces had absolutely lit up with the star sculpture.

The only real hiccup had come near the end when one of the caterers dropped a whole case of Champagne. Thankfully, the only person covered in the bubbly liquid was the young woman who'd rolled her ankle in a divot in the grass, sparing all the guests. Otto, of course, had eaten the cost and brought out another case from his van.

Alice nodded and took a sip of her wine. She'd convinced Brooke to drink the chilled white wine she had in the fridge instead of another bottle of Champagne. There had been plenty at the party.

"They seemed happy with the result," Alice admitted.

"Happy?" Brooke nearly shouted. "They looked like they were on the verge of tears the whole time and then—BAM! Final tarp comes off and their faces just exploded with smiles."

"Can you blame them?" Alice asked.

Brooke looked at her husband and she and Jared both shook their heads. It had been an insensitive comment. They'd lost their only child just six months ago. "Of course not. I'm sure they would give anything to have Peter back."

"So would I," said Alice. "Even this Inn."

A moment of silence passed where Brooke wasn't sure what to say. She was constantly considering Jared's mortality when in Alice's presence. Peter's passing had brought death closer to their family and it changed her perspective on living. In January, Brooke and Jared had increased their life insurance policies on each other—just in case. Having three young kids was not cheap, and to raise them on one income would be a challenge should something happen to one of them.

"The kids had—" she started, hoping to change the subject.

Alice interrupted, "But there's nothing that will bring him back so we'll all learn to live without him."

Another silence grew between the three adults until Jared finally asked, "Where's Celia? I thought you told me she was staying after, too."

Brooke nodded. She hadn't noticed Celia at the party but she hadn't really been focused on finding her, either. "I did tell you that." She turned to Alice. "I have no idea where she is. Do you?"

Alice shook her head, looking discouraged. "I didn't see her at all."

"I hope she's okay," Brooke said. "I didn't get a chance to call or text her yet." She pulled out her cell phone and sent a message off to their youngest sister. "I'm sure she's fine. Maybe something came up at work. I think she was having

Cori close the bookshop. That's a big responsibility for a high school senior."

Alice nodded but she didn't look convinced.

"Besides Celia not showing up and the Champagne incident, I thought the party was perfect. You were totally right to leave the star sculpture for last. I almost didn't let you make that change at the last minute," Brooke said, chuckling. "I'm glad I did."

"And what a surprise speech. I didn't know Peter was helping with the plans for the Inn. Did you?" Jared asked his wife.

"Only learned yesterday." Brooke sipped her wine and wished Celia would message back. Even just to let her know she was okay. She didn't need an explanation yet. Though she felt just as slighted as Alice did.

Brooke had poured hours of sweat and tears into tonight, as she did for all of her events. All she wanted was for everyone who mattered to Alice to be there to celebrate. Celia missing it was a big deal.

A knock on the door made all three adults look at each other in surprise. "Celia?" Brooke asked.

Alice shook her head. "Probably Marci. She had to go home to let her dogs out." She got up to let Marci inside.

"What do you think is going on with Celia?" whispered Jared when Alice had left the room.

Brooke shrugged. "Last night there was definite tension between Alice and Celia because Celia hasn't told Alice about Mitch." Jared's jaw dropped. "I know. I told Alice this afternoon. I shouldn't have, but I can't just let them turn their backs on each other. Alice softened toward her once she knew the truth."

Alice led Marci into the sitting room and Brooke and

Jared both stood. "Congratulations," Jared told her. "I love all the sculptures."

"Thank you," Marci said, leaning in for a quick hug. "And thank you, Brooke, for making tonight possible." She gave Brooke a much longer hug.

"It was my pleasure." Brooke loved her job. She just wished that all of her clients were as easy to work with. Of course, when she worked for free, that appreciation was easier to come by. But still. She'd had clients not pay her after the fact, claiming emotional damage because of some minor issue that Brooke would then bend over backward to fix. Alice and Marci were a breath of fresh air.

Everyone took their seats and started rehashing the event. This was one of Brooke's favorite parts of her job—reliving each success and learning how she could improve for the next one.

"I didn't know Greg was going to be there," Marci said.

Brooke rolled her eyes. "It was total last minute. He always does this—waits until the day before an event to RSVP, like he's waiting for something better to come along."

"Better?" Marci teased, taking her first sip of the wine Alice brought her.

"Everyone knows Brooke is the go-to event planner in Golden Bay. Her parties are not to be missed," Alice agreed.

"I don't know. Tell that to Golden Bay Country Club. I usually plan at least four big events for them every year, with a smattering of smaller ones in between, and they won't confirm the next one," Brooke said. "I'm sure they just have a lot going on with the start of summer, but these aren't little shindigs. If they want their Labor Day golf tournament to be as big as in the past, I have to get moving on it. Like, last week!"

"Maybe after tonight's success they'll see the light,"

Marci teased. "No one could have pulled off a better evening."

"Well, the weather certainly cooperated," Brooke admitted. "Perfect temperature, just enough wind to keep any bugs away, beautiful sunset. It was perfect, wasn't it?" Brooke relaxed in the memory of tonight.

"It was," Alice agreed. "Thank you, Brooke."

Brooke turned to her sister. There was a hint of seriousness in her voice that caught her attention. Her thank you was sincere. "Of course. I was happy to do it."

"Well, to show my appreciation, I'd like to offer you and Jared a weekend at the Inn this summer."

Brooke turned to her husband. "We have been talking about time away from the kids." She could feel excitement grow inside her at the thought of alone time. They loved their kids—Tina at ten was gaining her independence and sometimes actually becoming helpful, while Noah at six and Emma at four still demanded much of their time. But it had been years since Brooke and Jared had focused on each other for more than a few hours. Unlike when they'd first met in their senior year of college when they'd had all the time in the world to spend on each other. The years between college and kids had been filled with lazy weekends, late nights, and pampering each other whenever they wanted. The last ten had been a different story. Still fun—Brooke wouldn't trade her family for anything—but she'd sure enjoy a weekend alone with Jared.

"I bet Mom and Dad would babysit," Alice said suggestively. "If they ever come back."

Brooke could hear another layer of disappointment in Alice's voice. Not only had Celia missed tonight, but Mom and Dad had, too. It hadn't been a surprise, but Brooke was also miffed that they hadn't put in a bigger effort to be here.

"I'll let you know," Brooke said.

"Of course we'll take it," Jared said at the same time. He turned to his wife. "If your parents can't babysit, maybe Celia will be able to. The kids are old enough now that she'd be fine."

Everyone knew about Celia's apprehension about taking care of babies. Brooke had always made sure that when Celia babysat Emma that the baby was asleep when she got there and Brooke or Jared was home when she was ready for her next bottle or diaper. They'd gotten lucky with Emma—she'd been the easy baby.

"Thank you," Brooke said to Alice. "That's very thoughtful."

Marci reached into the bag at her feet then, a bag Brooke hadn't even noticed. "And to show my appreciation, I'd like to give this to you." She handed over a metal sculpture.

Brooke took it and turned to Jared. The sculpture was all black and made of five figures. There were two large ones, a medium one, and two smaller ones. Each vaguely resembled the shape of a human. The arms on the larger ones encircled the smaller ones, holding them close. Brooke thought of her family of five.

"This is incredible," she said to Marci. She couldn't stop smiling with joy.

"Thanks for making this all happen." Marci smiled back at her. "It was a perfect evening, and not just because of the weather," she teased.

Just then, Jared's phone rang. He leaned forward to grab it off the coffee table.

"It's Rebecca," he said, standing to take the call in the kitchen.

"Who's Rebecca?" Alice whispered as he left the room.

"The babysitter," Brooke told her, not really paying attention. It was after eight o'clock. All the kids should have been in bed by now. Brooke always imagined Rebecca flipping through the TV channels, sprawled on their couch, snacks from their cupboard in hand. Crumbs always showed up in the living room the day after she babysat. But she was fine with that since all the kids loved her.

Brooke kept one ear trained on the kitchen, trying to glean any information from Jared's side of the conversation. She didn't have to wait long before he came back to the sitting room. Brooke knew from the look on his face that something was wrong.

"Tina got up to ask Rebecca for water and fell down the stairs. She's not sure if Tina broke her arm."

Brooke stood, ready to leave with her husband, but he waved her back into her seat.

"We don't both have to go. You stay and enjoy the rest of the night with Alice and Marci. Get an Uber home." He gave her wineglass a pointed look. "We'll get the car in the morning. I'll go see how Tina is. If we go to the hospital, I'll call."

Brooke stood again and kissed Jared. He was always cool and calm in a crisis, much like herself. But it was hard to relinquish control completely. "I can meet you there if you need."

"Just enjoy your night," he told her, and gave her another kiss.

Then he turned to Alice, who had also stood. "Congratulations on the opening of the North Star Inn. Peter would be proud," he said, then wrapped her in a hug.

"Thanks for the sculpture, Marci," he said as he waved and left all three women looking after him.

Brooke knew she wasn't going to enjoy the rest of the

night like she could have without the call from Rebecca, but she would try. She glanced to her phone again, hoping Celia would have responded by now, but the screen just gave her the time when she pressed the button. She'd stay another hour, then get an Uber home so Rebecca wouldn't be there too late if Jared had to take Tina to the hospital.

"Do you think Tina's okay?" Alice asked.

Brooke wasn't sure if that was the first time she asked. She'd totally spaced out. Alice looked worried when Brooke finally looked up. "I hope so. She starts summer swim team next week. It'd be tough with a cast on."

"So what's this about Golden Bay Country Club not wanting you for their next golf tournament?" Marci asked, obviously trying to change the subject. "I'd be happy to write you a letter of recommendation, if you think that would help."

Brooke appreciated the effort to take her mind off of Tina, but she couldn't focus. She knew Jared could handle this, but she almost wished he'd asked her to help.

She turned toward Marci and Alice to find them both staring at her. She waved her hand in front of her face, like there had been a fly. "I don't think a letter of recommendation would help at this point. I've worked with them for so long they know my work. And they know that no one can do it better. At least not in Golden Bay. And I can't see them looking outside of town for another event planner."

"Could it be your fees?" Alice asked. "Not that you're not worth the cost, but you are on the high end, aren't you?"

Brooke smiled. "Of course I am. Nothing comes for free in this world—you know that, Alice. And if you want quality, you have to pay for it. What are you charging for a night here?" Brooke wanted to make her point.

Yes, she charged for her services. But no, she didn't

think they were unfair. And Alice was charging more than any other place in Golden Bay to stay at the North Star Inn.

But for good reason. Guests would have a beautiful and peaceful location for their stay, a private lawn and beach down to Lake Champlain, access to the new sculpture garden, abundant activities, and delicious food.

Likewise, when Brooke was hired to plan an event, clients received top-notch service including all the connections Brooke had cultivated over the years. Catering, flowers, music—there was nothing Brooke couldn't get, even at the last minute.

"Touché," Alice said, smiling. "You're right. It won't be cheap to stay here, but then I don't expect for everyone to be attracted to it. I'm looking for a certain type of guest, just like you and your clients."

Brooke nodded, barely paying attention to the conversation anymore. Her mind was on her phone. She wanted to hear from both Celia and Jared, even though he was probably barely home.

The conversation swirled around her until Brooke felt it wasn't rude to say her goodbyes. Marci took the opportunity to call it a night as well and offered to bring Brooke home. It was out of her way but would be faster than waiting for an Uber, so Brooke selfishly accepted.

She was somehow able to make small talk while they drove and was relieved to find a light on and no extra car in the driveway when Marci left her at home. Jared was finishing dishes in the sink when Brooke entered.

"No broken bones," he told her, not even turning around. They knew each other so well that he would have recognized her footsteps.

"That's a relief. Did you pay Rebecca for the time she

was expecting?" Brooke asked, taking a seat at the kitchen table.

Jared nodded. "She tried to give it back, though. She felt terrible for making me rush home for nothing. But Tina was really upset."

"That's fair. I'm sure she was shaken." Brooke put her cell phone on the table in front of her and found no texts. She sent another one to Celia, asking her to please respond. What was going on with her? She could have, at the very least, let Brooke or Alice know that she wouldn't make it tonight.

"Did you enjoy the rest of the night?" Jared asked.

Brooke looked up and saw him watching her. They had a rule about not using cell phones at the table. They were trying to model good behavior to their kids, and Brooke was the worst at breaking her own rules. She always used work as an excuse.

"As much as I could. I wish you'd texted to let me know Tina was okay. And I haven't heard back from Celia." Brooke opened her email, thinking there could be something in there.

Jared turned back to the sink and put the last of the day's dishes in the dishwasher, turning it on and sitting across from Brooke. "I'm sure she had something come up at work, just like you said."

Brooke nodded. "I know. She just needs to work on her communication. She doesn't realize people depend on her. We were counting on her. This was a big deal for Alice. And for me, too."

Brooke felt like she was on the verge of whining. She took a deep breath and continued.

"She just complains to me that Alice treats her like the

baby of the family still, but Celia plays the part far too often."

Jared didn't take his eyes off of Brooke but she had nothing left to say. He patted her hands that rested next to her phone and said, "I'm going up to shower. I'll see you in bed."

Brooke nodded. "Good night."

Her husband got up and Brooke looked to her phone. She had seven emails. Nothing from Celia, but one from Donna at Golden Bay Country Club, the Events Manager.

Brooke tapped her phone to open it and immediately regretted it. There would be no sleep for her tonight.

CHAPTER SIX

Celia stood in front of the bedroom's bookshelf, looking from book to book. More than half of them were books that Mitch had acquired over the years. History books. Landscaping books. Gardening. Fiction. Lifestyle. She was unwilling to pack his things into boxes. That felt like giving up on him. On them.

This was *their* home. They shared it. Why couldn't he see that their lives were intertwined and walking away wasn't as simple as just walking away? This was worth fighting for. And she wouldn't stop fighting for their love.

When she'd hung up on him outside Celia's Bookshelf this afternoon, Celia hadn't biked to Alice's. She'd meant to. But she was too upset at Mitch to pretend to have a good time. She wanted him to care about them the way she did. All she saw was indifference.

She knew she'd hear about missing Alice's party sooner rather than later. She shouldn't have skipped the launch party. She'd hear from both Brooke and Alice. And probably their parents, too.

Instead, Celia had biked to her lawyer's office.

She hated that she even needed a lawyer. A divorce lawyer. Mr. Williams. He looked like he could be her grandfather, with eyebrows that offered more shade than a sunhat. The first time she met him, Celia had wondered how many divorces he'd overseen. What a sad job, she'd thought.

But she'd hired him, anyway, two months ago when she was served divorce papers. She hadn't known where to look besides Google, and she wanted something more trustworthy than an online search. That was the only reason Brooke even knew her marriage was in such a sad state. Celia had told her Mitch had moved out right away, but hadn't intended to tell her he'd filed for divorce. Until she wanted a recommendation for a lawyer.

Celia hadn't trusted going to anyone but Brooke for that.

Not that Brooke would have personally used Mr. Williams's services, but a friend had. Two, actually.

"Divorce isn't the end of the world," Brooke had told her when Celia had burst into tears late at night at her house.

"It's the end of the world to me," Celia had sobbed. She was heartbroken. Even if her marriage wasn't perfect, she didn't want it to end. She loved Mitch. And she knew Mitch loved her. Or, at least, he had until some unexplained event may have changed that.

The difference now seemed to be that she was willing to work on it. She couldn't imagine waking up alone every morning. Even if she'd been doing it for four months now.

"We know plenty of people who have gotten divorced," Brooke had said, trying to make Celia feel better.

"But I'm not supposed to be one of them!" Celia had shouted back, storming out of Brooke's kitchen before she woke the kids or Jared came in, wondering what the shouting was about.

Celia had pedaled hard to Mr. Williams's office after talking to Mitch to look at the papers again. She wouldn't even keep them at home. She wanted nothing to do with them. She only wanted Mitch back. The Mitch she fell in love with and married six years ago.

The Mitch who got up early and had coffee ready for her every morning.

The Mitch who never forgot her birthday or their anniversaries—the anniversary of their meeting and the anniversary of their wedding.

The Mitch who always offered to drive when they went somewhere because he knew Celia hated driving.

The Mitch who surprised her last Christmas with new cross-country skis. Skis that had gotten plenty of use last winter when she would put them on every time she couldn't talk to Mitch because he'd moved out. That had been nearly every morning in February and March before Celia's Bookshelf was open for the day, and sometimes after work, too.

"Mrs. Randall," Mr. Williams said, when his secretary had let her into his office. "What can I do for you?"

He'd tried to stand to greet her but she waved her hand at him. She always worried that his knees would give out. "Don't get up. And please, it's Celia." She'd told him that every time she came to see him, but still he always called her Mrs. Randall. Maybe it was just his age, making him old-school. He never asked her to call him Ken.

There was a single chair across the desk from him, making it clear what he did. And what he didn't do. He didn't expect couples to come in together.

"Mitch called this afternoon," she told him. "I wanted to go over the paperwork again."

Mr. Williams nodded slowly and pulled her file out of his desk drawer. "Are you ready to sign?" he asked.

Celia shook her head. "No."

"It's a good deal he's offering you. The condo. Alimony. Cash—"

Celia held up her hand, cutting him off. She'd heard it all already. From Mr. Williams. From Brooke. Even from Jared, when Brooke had told him everything. "I feel like he's trying to buy his way out of this marriage."

Mr. Williams nodded again. She knew he'd heard it all before. And not just from her. This wasn't his first rodeo, but it was likely one of his last.

"Are you married, Mr. Williams?" Celia asked.

He smiled and leaned back in his chair. "Why do you ask?"

"Because if you've never been divorced, how can you possibly know how hard it can be?"

His smile widened and he leaned forward, his arms coming to rest between them on the desk. "I've been in this business a long time, Celia. I'm sure you've noticed that you're not my first client. It's not my intention to drive people apart. I've never felt that I've caused a divorce that wasn't my own—yes, I've been divorced. But I can help make the best of a lousy situation. And what Mitch is offering, I can assure you, is the best you could hope for. I don't see divorce as the end. It's a new beginning. For both of you. And it's up to you what you choose to do with this opportunity." He paused, letting Celia digest that. "Now, we could go to court. We could fight for more. Split his retirement savings. His business income for the next three years. Dig up any assets you might not know about. But would that really make a difference here? You have everything you need, or so you've said."

Celia's stomach twisted. The last thing she wanted was to go to court. What she wanted was for Mitch to come home to her. To at least give it another shot. If, at the end, he still wanted out, so be it. But he wasn't even trying.

"You're right. I'll get back to you," she said, standing.

Celia had waved to Mr. Williams's secretary on the way out, not even looking at the woman. She didn't want her to see her tears.

When her bike was unlocked and her helmet secured back on her head, Celia pulled out her cell phone. It was quarter to five. She had no idea where the time had gone.

There were two options now: show up to Alice's as she was—underdressed and sweating from biking around Golden Bay—or go home to shower and change before driving there. Either way, she'd be late and would miss the unveiling of the sculptures. She'd miss the speeches, probably already had.

Celia picked a third option—skip the launch party altogether.

So she'd ended up at home, eating leftovers straight from the container. Cold. Alone. Again.

Now, all Celia wanted was to call Brooke. But she couldn't, knowing that she was supposed to be with her at Alice's. Instead, she played both sides of the conversation she imagined having with her sister as she aimlessly walked through her condo, reminded constantly of who was missing.

Mr. Williams is right, this is a chance at a new beginning, Celia imagined Brooke saying.

I don't want a new beginning, Celia shot back. She just wanted her husband.

Celia's cell phone buzzed on the kitchen counter and she put down her dinner to see who it was. Brooke's ears must have been burning because she'd texted. *Where are you?*

Celia didn't respond. Her sister might have been the only person she wanted to talk to right now, but she knew Brooke was busy with Alice. And Celia was supposed to be with them.

So much for helping clean up after the party to make up to Alice for her coldness the night before. Now she owed her even more.

Rather than responding to Brooke, Celia shot a quick message to Cori to make sure closing went okay. She heard back immediately. *No problem. See you tomorrow afternoon.*

One less thing to worry about.

Celia left her phone on the kitchen counter again, knowing that the one person she wanted to talk to wasn't going to call. She sat down in front of the TV and flipped through channels, not finding anything exciting enough to draw her mind in and away from the constant torment of Mitch not being there.

After several half-hearted attempts and watching various shows, a tear slid down her cheek. Today's conversation with Mr. Williams felt different. It felt like the end. Her lawyer was trying to make her see what everyone else seemed to know. Celia refused to believe that their marriage was beyond saving.

They may not be close to where their relationship had started, but Celia was willing to start over. Give them another chance. A clean slate. Clear the air of whatever drove Mitch away.

Celia's mind wandered back to the start of their relationship as she sat in her lonely condo. Mitch had taken Celia to an amusement park on their first date. She'd been skeptical. At twenty-four, she loved going to them, but she wasn't about to admit that to a man she was interested in dating.

But he'd liked to have just as much fun as she did.

It had been a blind date, set up by a mutual friend neither of them had kept in touch with. By the time they'd married four years later, the friend had moved and they'd lost touch with him. They'd still toasted him on their honeymoon and every anniversary. If it hadn't been for him, they wouldn't have enjoyed their four years of dating and six years of marriage.

At the amusement park, Mitch and Celia had spent far more time waiting in lines than on any ride, but it had given them plenty of opportunity to get to know each other. They'd chosen only the twistiest and fastest roller coasters—Celia wanted to see if Mitch could keep up with her. He could. And then some. She'd had to call it quits first, after she ate two pieces of pizza and almost lost them after the next ride.

"I guess we won't be going whale watching or deep-sea fishing for our second date," Mitch had teased.

His sense of humor had made her smile through her queasiness.

"I'll just fast. I'm not going to let an upset stomach slow me down. Give me half an hour, then I'll be ready for another ride."

They'd walked around the park while she sipped water, learning about their families. She learned that he had an older brother, Stuart; that their parents had started a garage when the boys were kids, hoping at least one of them would take it over. Stuart didn't like getting his hands greasy, and Mitch wanted to spend more time outside than in a smelly garage. The garage was still open, but his parents had given up on the idea of either son taking it over now that Stuart and Mitch had their own endeavors.

Even while Celia pretended to watch TV alone, she thought back to that first date with fondness. The newness of the relationship had been so exciting. Maybe she could find that excitement again.

Maybe.

Celia's phone rang and she stood. She knew it wouldn't be Mitch. If it was Brooke or Alice, she wouldn't answer. Her right foot was asleep and she tripped as she headed toward the kitchen, then took a moment to shake some more blood to her lower extremity. When she reached the kitchen again, she'd missed the call. The phone rang again and she picked it up to see who it was.

It wasn't Brooke. Or Alice. Or Mitch.

"Hi," she said, not really ready for this call, either, but feeling guilty enough to answer.

"Celia," her mom said, sounding far too cheery.

"How's South Carolina?" she asked. If she planned the conversation right, she could avoid telling her mom why she was home rather than at Alice's. Her parents felt guilty about missing the event so maybe her mom wouldn't bring it up.

"We're in Virginia. Finally got the RV fixed and left this morning. I just wish it had come in a couple days earlier. Then we would have made it to Alice's opening."

"That's great." Unlike Brooke and Alice, Celia hadn't been bothered that her parents missed Alice's party. She'd been keeping the truth about her marriage from her parents, just as she had been from Alice. It was far easier to keep it a secret when they were out of state and she only talked to them every couple of weeks.

"Aren't you at Alice's?" her mom asked. "I tried Brooke and Alice but they weren't answering. Where are you?"

Celia felt only slightly hurt that she was her mother's last choice to call. She also considered lying and saying she was at Alice's, just taking a moment away from the crowd to enjoy the view. But the lie would never hold.

Not only was she a terrible liar, but her parents would hear the truth from Brooke and Alice at some point.

"Something came up," Celia said.

Her mom took it in stride, not asking more questions. Her mother was patient. She knew that the more she probed, the more her daughters withheld. Good thing she wasn't on the phone with her dad—he must have been driving. He was always better at picking up on his daughters' emotions, even through the phone. He could get to the bottom of a dark mood better than anyone she knew. In another life, he could have been a therapist.

"Well, we're coming home now that everything is fixed and we'd like to celebrate Alice's opening since we're missing the party tonight. I thought Saturday would be perfect. We should get home late afternoon and we could go straight to the Inn. We're so excited to see it."

Celia tuned her mother out as she caught sight of her wedding photo. Their anniversary was just a month away and she knew Mitch wouldn't forget it.

"Saturday?" Celia asked. "I think Alice has guests. It's her opening weekend."

"We can pick up dinner then. We are dying to see everyone. How's Mitch?" Her mom didn't wait for an answer. "And we can't wait to see how much Tina, Noah, and Emma have grown. Saturday, then."

"Mom—" Celia had to tell her the truth about Mitch. At least over the phone she wouldn't have to see her mother's disappointment. She could be quicker if they weren't in the same room.

"What's wrong with Saturday?" her mom asked.

"Nothing." Celia waited for her mom to fill in the silence. It didn't happen. "It's not about that. But—Mitch moved out. He asked for a divorce."

Celia's mom was speechless, something that didn't happen often.

"Celia?" her dad suddenly asked. "Are you okay?"

"Are you driving?" Celia asked. It was dark outside and she didn't want her dad talking to her on the phone while driving.

"No. We're stopped for the night. Mom just handed me the phone. What's going on?" His voice was full of concern and Celia suddenly regretted not telling him sooner.

"Mitch left me." She could feel the tears coming again as she held her wedding photo. She wished for the millionth time tonight that Brooke was available.

"Oh, Celia. We would have come home sooner if we'd known. We didn't know you were having trouble."

"Of course you didn't. You couldn't have. I didn't tell you." Celia should have told him.

"Are you okay? Do you need anything?" he asked.

"I'm okay. But I could use a drink." Celia and her dad laughed.

"Did this just happen?"

Celia left the couch and looked out her sliding door over her deck. She could just barely see the lake in the distance. "No. He filed two months ago. I'm sorry I didn't tell you," she whispered.

"You have nothing to be sorry about," he reassured her.

When her dad didn't say anything else, Celia continued, "Tell Mom Saturday is fine for dinner with everyone.

At least, for me. I'll be there. I'm sure Alice and Brooke will make time to see you, too. We've all missed you guys and we're glad you're finally coming back."

She was ready to say goodbye when he asked, "Are you sure you're okay?"

Celia kept her eyes focused on the distant lake. She was barely okay, but there was nothing her dad could do from Virginia in his RV. They were a two-day drive away.

And there was nothing anyone could do. This was all up to Celia and Mitch. It was her life. Her marriage on the line. Her future with her husband, the man of her dreams, in question.

Mr. Williams's words rang in her head again. *It's a new beginning. For both of you. And it's up to you what you choose to do with this opportunity.*

Before she could stop it, the truth slipped out. "No. I'm not okay. Not right now. That's why I didn't go to Alice's launch party. I just couldn't face so much happiness. But I will be okay."

Celia could almost hear her dad smile through his words. "I know you will be. Good night, Celia."

"Drive safe. I'll see you Saturday."

Before she could hang up, her mom got back on the phone. "I love you," she said.

"I love you, too, Mom." Celia hung up and looked toward the sky. Stars were starting to come out.

As she watched, a car she didn't recognize drove into the condo's parking lot. It was only a tri-plex, so it was easy to know the neighbors and their habits. She and Mitch were the longest owners of the three units, inhabiting the westernmost condo. The middle unit had been empty for a couple months, and the furthest east was owned by an elderly couple. Celia knew them enough to greet them and share holiday cards, but they were hardly good friends. Neighborly, that's what they were.

But this car was not theirs. Their condo was usually dark by now.

Celia stood at her slider, knowing that she was perfectly visible to the world outside, back-lit from inside. A man about her age got out of the driver's seat, followed by a preteen from the passenger side. They each retrieved a bag from the backseat and headed toward the middle condo.

As the motion sensor lights turned on as they walked up the steps, the man looked at Celia and she gasped. She knew him.

The man waved and she waved back as she wracked her brain to remember his name. All she could do was remember his face.

It looked like she had new neighbors.

CHAPTER SEVEN

Alice rolled over as the light spilled through the windows. She didn't close the curtains anymore, waking with the sun earlier and earlier, the summer solstice just weeks away. This gave her an early start for making breakfast for guests.

This was her last morning alone at the North Star Inn. This afternoon, two couples would be arriving and Alice felt the anticipation building.

Before she sat up and put her feet down on the hardwood floors, she mentally went over what she wanted to accomplish this morning—last-minute checks on the two reserved rooms; inventory of the fridge; a stop at the farmer's market; and prepping for tomorrow's breakfast.

Now that it was here, Alice was nervous to be cooking for guests.

She filled her lungs and exhaled, then got out of bed, forcing the moment of insecurity to pass. The quiet of the morning was calming, and Alice made her way to the kitchen.

Alice's private living space was on the main floor,

hidden on the northeast side of the Inn. The kitchen was the only room accessible by both her private space and the rooms shared by her guests. She even had her own entrance around the side of the building so she could always enter and exit away from her guests if she wanted. She expected to use the sitting room on the west side more than her small living room, but was glad to have the privacy for when she wanted it.

Tomorrow's breakfast was going to be simple—eggs cooked to the guests' liking, thick slices of toast, and fruit. Everything would be fresh, and many of the ingredients still had to be purchased this morning at the Golden Bay farmer's market. There were just enough eggs in the fridge today for Alice to have a hearty breakfast to start the day on the right foot.

But before she did that, a cup of coffee was in order. Rather than using the Keurig she made available for self-service in the dining room, Alice heated water and took a French press to the screened porch to enjoy the morning sun.

Alice couldn't stop thinking about Celia skipping her launch party yesterday. It hurt. More than it should have after knowing her for thirty-four years. They'd never been the closest of sisters, but they seemed to be growing further apart.

She'd noticed it start when Celia was in high school. Alice was married with two young daughters by then and she seemed to have nothing in common with her youngest sister who never tried to find common ground.

Alice sighed. People didn't change, she reminded herself as the first sip of black coffee enlivened her senses. But Celia was family. And if there was one truth Alice lived by, it was that she stuck by family.

Alice shook her head and took her cup of coffee back to the kitchen to make breakfast. She glanced to her phone, hoping beyond hope that Celia would have messaged an apology.

There was nothing.

Alice accepted that, ate a filling breakfast, and showered, trying to wash away her annoyance.

Then it was down to business. She grabbed her list and shopping bags and headed to town on foot. A walk would help clear her mind and calm her nerves about this afternoon.

The farmer's market was setup every Friday and Saturday morning on a side street half a mile from the Inn. Alice started with a vendor she visited every week—Hope's Hens.

Hope was a friend of Viv's who raised free-range chickens for both eggs and meat. "Hi, Alice. You're here early," Hope said, a smile lighting up her face.

"Opening weekend," she said. All of her acquaintances knew how hard she'd worked for this day.

"Congratulations! I heard the launch party was a success. Everyone's talking about Marci's sculptures."

That made Alice happy. Word had already gotten around about the unveiling, and it had barely been twelve hours since the tarps had come off.

"First guests arrive this afternoon. I'll need more eggs than usual."

Hope had already put Alice's regular two dozen off to the side for Alice. "Of course. How many?"

"I'll take five dozen."

Hope's eyes widened. "Busy weekend?"

Alice chuckled. "Just two couples coming for two nights each. But I'd rather have too many than not enough. I can always bake with the extra for next weekend. I don't have many mid-week bookings yet. The Inn is still young."

Hope brought out three more dozen, then a half-dozen container. "Duck eggs," she said. "Save them for yourself. They're some of the first eggs I've gotten from my young flock."

"Thanks, Hope. It's been years since I had duck eggs." Alice and Peter had indulged in duck eggs before they'd had kids. But the cost had kept them away as their daughters had grown, and the cost of raising them had grown with them.

Everything still reminded Alice of Peter. Something as simple as duck eggs sent her heart lurching for what she could no longer have. A future that had been stolen from her. But had it really ever been hers? The future was always uncertain, and Alice had to look toward it instead of the past.

"I should start getting more any day. These are on me. An opening weekend gift." Hope gently placed the cartons in Alice's bag and accepted her money.

"Thanks again, Hope. Have you seen Viv recently?" Even though Alice and Viv were close, she sometimes got stories from Hope that she didn't get from Viv.

Hope shook her head. "No. She's too busy with the end of the school year. I'm sure she'll come by the farm soon, though. You know she's dating my neighbor, right?"

Alice was stunned. "I didn't know that."

Hope's hand shot to her mouth and her cheeks turned pink. "I probably wasn't supposed to tell you that."

Golden Bay was a small town. If Viv was dating someone, it was only a matter of time before Alice would find out. Viv had to know that by now.

"Aiden?" Alice asked.

Hope nodded. "They're good for each other, if you ask me."

"I don't know him well," Alice admitted. She only knew his name from Hope and Viv having talked about him. He'd moved to Golden Bay after Viv left for college and came back. Aiden was newer to town, and far younger than Alice's friends.

"Thanks for the eggs," Alice said to Hope. "And the news about Viv. I'll make sure to keep it under wraps."

Hope laughed. "I'm sure you would have found out sooner or later if Viv wasn't the one to tell you."

Alice silently agreed and waved. There was already a small crowd forming and Alice didn't want to slow down Hope's business. She knew how hard everyone worked as small business owners just to make ends meet. Farming was a tough career choice, but she was thankful for so many small farms in and around Golden Bay. She wouldn't eat half as well if she couldn't get such fresh, delicious ingredients.

Alice's next stop was Jake's Greens. Jake was a fourth generation Golden Bay resident and farmer. He had prime farmland, having inherited it from previous generations. Because of that, and because of his dedication to his farm, his veggies couldn't be beat.

"Alice," he called out before she'd even made eye contact with him down the row of vendors' tents.

She waved and walked over. "Morning, Jake."

"The North Star Inn is all the talk this morning," Jake stage whispered. His other customers glanced toward Alice and she felt her cheeks grow warm. "You really got everyone talking with Marci's sculptures."

Alice hadn't truly expected the sculptures to be such a surprise. Sure, no one would know what exactly they were until the tarps were removed. But what else could have been hidden under there? So she asked. "What did you think the tarps were hiding?"

"Trees."

Alice laughed. "Trees? Like, apple trees?"

Jake shrugged. "Apple. Pear. Oak. There were plenty of guesses. Personally, I thought they might be peach trees. With all the sun you get, they'd be less likely to be hit by late spring frosts. Maybe every one year out of four you'd get a peach harvest."

Another laugh escaped from Alice's mouth. "Peach trees. There's something I hadn't thought of."

"Well, once a farmer, always a farmer. I can't look at a piece of land and *not* imagine what would grow best there." Jake walked away to collect a payment, then returned to Alice. "What can I get you today?"

Alice looked around and filled her bag while Jake weighed and tallied. She handed over her money and thanked him for all his hard work at bringing the best produce to Golden Bay. "I don't know where I'd shop if you weren't here," she told him, receiving a wide smile in return.

"Have a great opening weekend," he said as she turned to head to her next stop.

Alice felt the weight growing on her arm and wondered if she should have driven. It wasn't a long walk, but she hadn't anticipated so many eggs. And she still had to buy bread and fruit.

She found Zelman's and was pleased to see early strawberries. They were still a few weeks away from the main crop, but with the mild winter and spring they'd experienced, the first ones were already ripening.

There was a large crowd vying for the first of the

summer's fruits, so Alice was quick, taking four pints of the delicious-looking fruit, and slipping back out of the crowd.

Now there was just one stop left before heading back to the Inn. Bread.

In the last six months, Alice had spent hours upon hours baking and cooking to help process Peter's death. Many of those hours had been spent trying new bread recipes. She wasn't confident enough yet to bake bread for her guests, and nothing she made came close to Heather's Breads and Pastries.

Alice had grown up with Heather in Golden Bay and had watched as her friend had gone from a small-time baker to one of national acclaim. Heather could hardly ever be found at the farmer's market, hiring teenagers to sell her products, but today Alice was surprised to see her there.

"Morning, Heather," Alice said. "What a pleasant surprise."

Heather turned around with two loaves of mouth-watering bread in her hands and placed them on top of the pile on the table. "Alice. Good to see you. I know. I hardly ever make it out here anymore. But Megan called out this morning, and then Ashley did too. This was only their second week, having just come back from college for the summer. I don't know if they're going to last." Heather rolled her eyes.

Alice was glad that she didn't have to hire employees. She'd heard plenty of horror stories from Celia and Heather over the years about teens' unreliableness. They might have offered affordable labor, but if you couldn't count on them to show up, were they really worth it?

"Well, your loss is my gain. I love seeing you here. Any new recipes you're trying?" Alice asked. She always offered to be a taste tester for Heather. Some had been better than others, but Alice always gave an honest review.

"Actually, yes. A whole wheat sourdough. It's as close to 'natural' as I've come. You know, the first breads are thought to be porridges that were forgotten in a corner where natural yeasts made the dough rise? Why someone then thought to bake it instead of tossing it is beyond me. But I guess if you don't know where your next meal is coming from, you'll get creative to see what can be saved."

Heather sliced a piece of bread, spread some soft butter on it, and handed it to Alice.

"Mmm," she said around the bread in her mouth. "It's so moist."

"That's the thing about sourdoughs. They make you salivate. We're made to eat sourdoughs. The long fermentation is what allows all the bacteria to make the nutrients of the whole wheat become bioavailable to us." Heather's hands flew through the air as she talked, animated and passionate about her work.

Alice took another bite, finishing the slice. "I'll take a loaf of this one. And a potato bread and ciabatta."

"Congratulations on opening," Heather said as Alice paid. "I bet that's a weight off your shoulders. Sometimes the anticipation is heavier than the work."

As Alice left with her bags loaded down, she thought about Heather's parting comment. Her friend was right. The build-up to today had been huge. While she still didn't have guests, she could already feel the weight coming off. Having guests couldn't be harder than updating the Inn.

She hoped.

Alice was lost in her thoughts of the coming weekend when she nearly bumped right into Will. "I'm so sorry," she said, almost dropping her bag of eggs.

"My fault," he assured her, steadying her with one hand. The other held a small box. "Congratulations on last night's party. I heard nothing but glowing reviews all night."

Alice remembered seeing him and Irene last night on the west lawn when she gave her speech. As Irene's older brother, Alice had known Will pretty much all her life, but never very well.

"I have some foraged mushrooms that I was going to offer Casey at Casey's Place but if you've never had them, they're worth trying." Will held out the box in his hand and Alice peered inside. What she saw did not look like food. They looked like small brains with stems.

"You do have to be careful with how you cook them, though. If they're not thoroughly cooked, they could kill you."

Alice laughed. "I think I'll pass, but thank you." She was touched that Will would offer her these apparently prized morels for free when he could probably earn a pretty penny from the fanciest restaurant in town.

Will nodded. "Good to see you, Alice. I have to go find Casey."

Alice walked back through the farmer's market and down the street to the Inn. She had everything she needed for tomorrow's breakfast. Now she just needed guests.

As Alice stepped inside, she heard her cell phone ringing in her back pocket. Her arms were too full to do anything about it, and by the time the bags were all on the counter, she'd missed the call. The missed call alert told her it was her parents.

Alice quickly called them back, hoping to catch them. After all the praise she'd received this morning, she wanted to bask in her successes a bit longer by telling her parents about last night.

"Hi Alice. I wasn't sure you were up yet," her mom said when she answered.

"I get up early," she reminded her mom. "Guests come this afternoon so I have to be ready to cook early breakfasts."

"I can't imagine they'll get up too early. They're on vacation, after all."

Alice smiled. Her parents were on one long vacation called retirement. They'd earned it. She was actually surprised to hear from them before noon. "How's the RV?" Alice asked, cradling the phone between her ear and shoulder, knowing she would pay for it with neck pain later.

"All fixed. We're on our way home. We wanted to celebrate with you tomorrow night. Dad and I are bummed that we missed last night's party. Celia already agreed to dinner at the Inn."

Alice's heart rate increased. She was bummed that her parents hadn't been there last night, too, but it didn't sting anymore. Their absence wasn't a surprise. Celia's was. But she did wish that she'd been consulted before making plans for a family dinner during her opening weekend.

"Oh," Alice said, feeling blind-sided. "You'll be back by then?"

"Your dad is driving now. Left Virginia this morning."

That explained why they were calling so early.

"So, dinner tomorrow then? We can't wait to see the finished product."

"Umm... can I get back to you about dinner? I have guests to take care of." Alice opened the fridge and found space for all of her eggs.

"You won't be serving them dinner, will you?"

Alice loved her mother. She'd given her the best life possible. She missed having her in Golden Bay during the winter, but she was caught so off guard with these plans that she couldn't commit yet.

"Well, no," Alice said. She just wanted to be available for anything that might come up.

"We'll pick up dinner. You don't even have to cook. Nepali?"

Alice smiled. Even she had to admit that if she wasn't cooking, having everyone together would be an enjoyable evening. "I just had it two nights ago with Celia and Brooke."

"Well, Thai then."

Alice sighed. "Okay. Five o'clock?" Other than having guests at the Inn for the weekend, Alice didn't have any other plans tomorrow.

"We'll be there. I'll let Celia and Brooke know. And can you get Viv and Nora there, too? We miss them."

Alice's parents were devoted grandparents. Even if this wasn't the Inn's opening weekend, they would have still wanted to get everyone together so they could see their grandkids.

"I'll do my best." Alice wrote on a scrap of paper to call her daughters to invite them to tomorrow's dinner and stuck it to the fridge. She wanted to try to get Viv to tell her about Aiden anyway, so this would be a good excuse to call.

"We'll see you tomorrow, then. Love you."

"Love you," Alice's dad called in the background.

"Love you, too. And drive safe," Alice said, then hung up.

She put the rest of her food away and started getting things out for lunch. After her big breakfast, she didn't need anything fancy. Hummus and crackers would fill her up just fine, with some fresh strawberries.

The berries were washed and Alice was ready to make a

plate when she heard tires crunching outside in the driveway. The clock told her that it was still far too early for guests. They weren't scheduled to arrive until at least three. But one glance toward the driveway told her that someone was here.

Alice abandoned her lunch plans for now and headed outside.

The only times Alice had spoken to her weekend guests —Stella and David, Astrid and Karl—had been on the phone. She had never seen their photos.

So when a man stepped out of the driver's door and looked toward the Inn, Alice could only assume it was either David or Karl. When no one exited the passenger side, though, Alice started questioning if this man was someone else.

"Hello," she called, walking down the steps toward the driveway. She would be friendly to him no matter what.

"Mrs. North?" he asked, heading in her direction.

Still, no partner joined him from the other side of the car and Alice didn't think he was a guest anymore.

"Yes." She stayed at the bottom of the steps, unsure of this man and what he wanted.

"I'm Mr. Thompson. I'm representing Jack and Linda Lewis. Would it be okay if I came in?"

Alice was silent. She was no longer hungry. This man certainly sounded like a lawyer. But why was he here? She'd tried to learn the names of her birth parents years ago and had only come up with first names—Jack and Linda. Was he here on their behalf today?

CHAPTER EIGHT

"Coffee?" Brooke asked Jared as their middle child bustled around them. Noah always seemed to jump out of bed at top speed, and Brooke needed at least two cups of coffee before she could even try to keep up with one kid.

"Please." Jared grabbed the milk from the fridge to top off his mug. "You're up early."

Brooke hadn't gone to bed last night until she knew Jared would be asleep. She didn't want to keep him awake with the tossing and turning she knew she'd do. The email from Donna had her blood boiling.

"Couldn't sleep." Brooke pushed bread down into the toaster, hoping it wouldn't be a battle to get her kids to eat this morning. She wanted to be out the door with Jared, not a minute after.

"Can you drop the kids off this morning?" he asked, taking a seat at the table.

Brooke stopped in her tracks. She took a deep breath, remembering that Jared didn't know about the email canceling a huge job. She counted on the country club's regular business. And they paid well.

"I can do Tina and Noah. Can you drop off Emma?" With the school year almost finished, the kids were all extra antsy to be done for the summer. Emma seemed to feel the excitement most keenly. Lately, whenever Brooke dropped their youngest off, there were tears and screaming. Jared seemed to have the magic touch to get in and out before Emma even noticed she was being left without her parents or siblings.

"I have a meeting at eight," he said.

Brooke had forgotten. "Okay. Then we have to get moving. My car's still at Alice's."

Jared cringed. "I forgot."

The kids' schools weren't far apart, drop-off was just extra time that Brooke wanted to have to convince Donna to take her back.

"You okay?" Jared asked, concern in his eyes.

Brooke nodded. She couldn't even look at her husband. "I heard from the country club last night. Donna sent an email. They chose a different event planner for the Labor Day golf tournament."

Jared's mug was stopped halfway to his lips when Brooke finally looked at him. "You're kidding."

They depended on Brooke's income far more than Jared's. His work as an independent children's book illustrator had grown more and more consistent as he'd made a name for himself and truly became a partner with the authors he worked with. But Brooke's paydays were far bigger. Especially with her quarterly events for the country club.

Brooke shook her head.

"Who?" Jared asked.

"I don't know. But I intend to find out. I'm going over there this morning to talk to Donna. I can't imagine they found someone better. Why would they even be looking? They've never had any complaints with my work." Brooke stopped herself from badmouthing a client she needed to woo back.

"We'll figure this out." Jared stood and went to the kids' bedrooms. "Breakfast," she heard him call to them.

Brooke got their toast ready and added sliced apples to their plates. If they finished even half of what she gave them, she'd consider it a success. They didn't like being shuffled out of the house this early.

Noah raced into his seat, practically bouncing out of it, while Tina and Emma looked like they'd barely woken up yet.

"How's your arm this morning?" Brooke asked Tina. She hadn't seen her kids awake last night but had made sure to give them each a kiss before she went to bed.

"Fine," her ten-year-old said. "It really hurt last night though."

"I'm glad it isn't broken," Brooke said, placing three plates on the table.

"We have to leave early today," Jared told them. "Mom's car is at Aunt Alice's." His news was met with groans from three kids. Then he turned to Brooke and said, "I'm going to finish getting ready. I packed the kids' bags with them last night. Can you do their lunchboxes?"

Brooke wanted to sit down and drink her coffee while her kids ate, but she went back to the kitchen instead. "Sure."

She'd already showered and dressed for the day. The shower had helped take away some of the exhaustion from her night of almost no sleep, and the coffee was definitely helping there too. But she knew it'd be a tiring afternoon.

Brooke checked the time as she tossed bags into lunchboxes, making sure each kid had only foods they'd eat—Emma flat out refused carrots, but they were the only vegetable Noah would eat; Tina only liked peanuts while Emma only ate cashews. It was a constant juggling act, and the balls didn't always stay in the air.

They only had fifteen minutes until they had to be buckled into Jared's car. She double checked their bags and found everything there, then added the lunchboxes as Tina finished breakfast and cleaned up her dishes.

Brooke reminded the kids to brush their teeth just as Jared returned, looking stressed. With two minutes to spare, they were in the car and Brooke was double checking seat-belts while she replayed last night's email in her head. She could get the kids in the car on autopilot and think about something else completely.

The drive to Alice's was full of chatter from the back-seat while Brooke and Jared retreated into their coming days. Jared gave everyone a kiss when Brooke and the kids switched cars, and then he was off. "You'll rock it," Brooke told him, like every time he met with a new potential partner.

"Emma first," Brooke said as they pulled up by the preschool minutes later. She unbuckled her daughter, who happily jumped out of the car with a wave to her older siblings. Brooke was surprised as they walked inside the building that Emma ran ahead of her into her classroom without even a backward glance. Brooke was quick to stow away Emma's lunch in the fridge, then waved to the teacher before leaving.

"That was quick," Tina commented when Brooke got back into the car. "Even faster than when Dad drops her off."

Brooke shook her head, her eyes wide in surprise. "I

didn't expect that," she admitted, appreciating the small unexpected success in her morning.

She then dropped off her older kids without even having to get out of the car. She missed the days when they needed her more but also relished their independence.

Finally, Brooke turned the car west toward Golden Bay Country Club, playing her opening argument over in her mind.

There were plenty of cars already in the parking lot at this hour in the morning. Being right on the water, the club's busiest season was in full swing. They had canoes, kayaks, and even sailboats for taking out on Lake Champlain, in addition to the golf course and driving range, tennis courts, pickleball, and small playground.

Brooke and her family wouldn't be members if she didn't get a steep discount as their go-to event planner. But with the recent change, she wasn't sure they'd be able to spend their summer canoeing and kayaking and swimming here like they usually did.

The receptionist recognized Brooke and waved as she walked confidently past. "Donna in?" she called over her shoulder. This was her usual greeting, but she was usually here to discuss the next event's plans. Not to beg her way back into a job.

"Yup. Just back from her morning tee time."

Good thing I dropped the kids off, Brooke thought. Otherwise she'd have been forced to wait here for Donna to finish her round of golf.

Brooke knocked on the open door to Donna's office and walked inside.

"Brooke," Donna said, looking up from her computer. "Good morning. Have a seat."

Brooke was happy to see that she'd flustered the woman.

She hadn't expected Brooke to show up uninvited. An email back, perhaps, but not showing up on her doorstep first thing Friday morning.

"Thanks," Brooke said, and sat down. "I got your email."

"I thought you would have." Donna leaned back in her chair and took a deep breath. Brooke had her totally off-guard.

"It was quite a surprise," Brooke admitted, crossing her legs and leaning forward. She was on the offensive.

"I fought tooth and nail for you. But the board wanted to go with someone else," Donna said.

Brooke wasn't sure if this was a good thing or not. Donna might just be the messenger and have no power to change anything. She nodded slowly. "Who?" she asked.

Donna looked away. "You know I shouldn't be telling you that."

"Then tell me as a friend. We are friends, right? I'm a customer interested in coming to the tournament and I want to know what to expect. If Brooke Hastings was organizing it, I'd be sure to buy a ticket. Maybe even splurge on two. But without her, I don't know what to expect."

Donna smiled. "Brooke..." she started, but let it trail off into nothing.

"Who is it, Donna?" Brooke asked quietly.

There was a long pause but Brooke knew Donna would tell her. Their history was too long not to.

Donna took a deep breath and looked past Brooke before telling her, "Stuart."

"Stuart Randall?" Brooke was shocked, leaning back in her chair as if Donna's single word had blasted her. "All the way from Burlington?"

Donna shrugged. "Like I said, I fought for you to keep

the job. I didn't want to lose you. And I wanted to keep it all local. He won't know Golden Bay like you do."

Brooke still couldn't speak. It wasn't that they'd hired someone from Burlington to plan their next Labor Day golf tournament. It was that they'd hired Mitch's brother to plan it.

"The only thing I could get the board to agree to," Donna continued, "was to have you two work together and keep you on as a contractor."

Brooke looked up, ready to refuse. She was already an independent contractor. This would just mean the club would have more control over how much money she made.

"Before you say no, consider that you'd have less work. You could just do the parts you like the best. And maybe you'd make new connections in Burlington. You could expand there." Donna's words fell out of her mouth at top speed, like she was trying to get everything out before Brooke stopped her.

Donna was obviously trying to make the best of a decision she hadn't agreed with. And keep Brooke around for future events. Brooke needed them more than they needed her, apparently.

She shook her head anyway. "If I wanted to expand or make new connections in Burlington, I could do that. Thanks, but no thanks."

"Brooke—"

"How much lower did he ask?" Brooke asked before Donna could beg her to work for practically nothing.

There was another long silence before Donna said anything. "I can't say."

Donna's pause had Brooke thinking this was all about the money. "A thousand? Two? Am I getting pushed out over a few thousand dollars?" Brooke shot, lowering her voice halfway through her accusation. "The club must be hurting if that's all it takes."

"It wasn't his fees," Donna admitted, looking away. "Well, I'm sure that was part of it. But it wasn't the main sticking point."

Brooke raised her eyebrows. The country club had never offered her anything but glowing feedback. If there had been complaints about her work, she didn't know about them.

"What, then? I've done all of your biggest events for years. What is he offering that I can't deliver?" Brooke asked.

Donna looked everywhere except at Brooke. But Brooke wasn't going to back down. If she lost this tournament, she'd probably lose the other three events the country club hired her for annually. That would mean nearly halving her income. She couldn't afford for that to happen.

"His quote was $20,000 below yours."

Brooke's stomach twisted. How was that possible?

If it was just a thousand or two, she could have fought her way back into the club's good graces. But $20,000? There was no way she could put together the same kind of event with that steep discount.

"He promised quality," Donna said. "And he had glowing recommendations from some of his partners he keeps on retainer."

"He doesn't work alone, does he?" Brooke asked. She was a one-woman show and loved it that way. She knew it also meant that she was a small fish in a big dog world.

Donna shook her head. "He's part of a national company. But his partnerships are all local."

Brooke nodded. She couldn't say no anymore. Not if Stuart was going to snatch up her big clients and leave her with his leftovers. The country club was just the first. "Okay. I'll work with him. If you can tell me what that will look like."

Donna smiled. "Excellent. I haven't told Stuart yet that we're going with his proposal, so we can work you into the contract."

That made Brooke feel even worse. She'd been rejected before Stuart had even accepted the job. This was worse than she'd thought.

Donna slid the club's proposal across the desk for Brooke to study. "I'll leave you to look it over. Coffee?"

Brooke accepted. A third cup would get her through her afternoon.

While Donna left the office to get coffee, Brooke read the contract. She was already written into it. She'd receive seventy percent of her regular fees. She had to accept.

Donna came back and set a coffee in front of Brooke. "I'll work with Stuart," Brooke told her. "But you have to promise that you won't just cut me out of the tree lighting." The December event kicked off the holiday season and Brooke would need that income.

"I'll do my best," Donna told her, sitting across from her again. "I promise to fight for you with the board. But they're always looking at the bottom line. I'm looking at the customer experience first. And I know you deliver. We'll see how this one goes. Then maybe we can get you on retainer."

Brooke had proposed this very scenario in the past but had always been met with resistance. The same excuse she heard today—the board. Brooke believed that Donna did her best to keep Brooke working for them, but there was only so much one person could do. The golf tournament would be her chance to prove that she was worth a retaining fee.

"And we have some smaller events planned this summer and fall that we'd love to talk to you about," Donna said, almost sounding like she was trying to appease Brooke.

She nodded. "Okay. Send off your contract to Stuart first. See what he says." She wasn't going to commit to anything until she knew what the golf tournament was going to look like.

The two women shook hands and Brooke left with her coffee. She had the sinking feeling that it might be time for her to look for bigger clients elsewhere.

CHAPTER NINE

Celia woke early Friday morning. Her first thought was of Mitch. Everyone morning, her first thought was of Mitch. All Celia wanted was to wake up next to him again.

It was time to take action. No more of this divorce business. She and Mitch were married, and she intended to keep it that way.

First things first, though. She had to apologize to Alice for last night. She hadn't even responded to Brooke's text asking if she was okay. And Alice hadn't reached out.

Her sister was like that. Alice could wait. She had the patience of a saint, and Celia had to admit that she'd tested her limits over the years. Celia still hadn't found Alice's breaking point.

Sorry I missed last night's party. Come to lunch at the bookstore and I'll explain? Celia pressed send. It was time to tell her about Mitch moving out and filing for divorce.

Those weren't excuses for Celia's lack of dedication to Alice's opening. She should have gone. Alice had always supported her, and she owed it to her sister to do the same.

Like with her marriage, there was nothing to do but move forward. She just hoped she hadn't burned her bridge with Alice.

Celia showered and had breakfast, trying to think positively about her day. She had tomorrow morning's story time to get ready for. Hopefully Noah and Emma would come with Jared or Brooke. She loved having her niece and nephew there. Tina had outgrown Saturday morning story time at Celia's Bookshelf, but she'd been the reason Celia had started it.

When Tina was a baby, she'd been spoiled rotten by everyone. It had been years since Alice's kids were little, and Celia's parents were over the moon having a baby to dote on. And Celia was even old enough to appreciate Tina's tininess. She didn't want to take care of Tina, but she was happy to create a family activity for everyone in the early days of the bookstore. She'd even wanted to call it Tina's Story Hour. Brooke had vetoed and Celia was glad she had when Noah came along four years later.

Celia had planned to read about pirates tomorrow morning. She liked to pair her story time themes with the seasons, and summer was just starting. Books about boating, exploring, and being outside filled her list of ideas for Saturday's stories.

Now, instead of pirates, Celia was leaning toward being in the garden. She had some new books in that she could show off to the parents who came in with their little ones. Saturdays were her highest sales days, and having kids asking for picture books certainly helped.

Celia put her dishes away as her cell phone rang with a message. She hoped it was Alice agreeing to lunch with her. Instead, she was surprised to see a message from Mitch.

He'd barely said a word to her in the last four months, and now he was contacting her two days in a row.

Did you sign them? was all it said.

Enough was enough. This wasn't a conversation to have over texting. Celia called him.

To her surprise, Mitch answered right away.

"Celia." His voice was less than friendly but she didn't let that turn her away from him. She loved him; his good qualities and his less-than-perfect ones, too.

"Good morning," she said, hoping to lighten the mood.

Silence rang louder than thunder in her ear.

"I'm guessing you didn't sign them," Mitch said, his voice deadpan.

Celia was on high alert, looking for any sign as to why this request for a divorce had come up. That he wasn't able to show her any emotion told her that he was hiding his feelings. Did he even want this divorce?

"Of course not. You're worth keeping around."

The only reason Celia knew Mitch was still on the other end of the phone was his breathing.

"I was thinking about our first date last night. Remember how I almost lost my lunch?" Celia made herself laugh into the void. "That whole day, I thought I'd last longer on the roller coasters than you would."

Mitch sighed. "I remember." Celia wasn't sure, but she thought she heard a smile through his words.

"I want to keep riding roller coasters with you, Mitch. Real ones, but also the roller coaster of life." Tears stung the backs of her eyes. "I'll do anything to keep our marriage alive. I won't sign those papers."

Another sigh met Celia's ear, this one softer than the last.

She continued on. "I know you aren't interested in

counseling. But we could go on a couple's retreat. Or just on vacation. Take a week off. I know that's hard, especially with the start of the summer landscaping season. But you're worth it to me. I can close for a week. Or see if I can piece together enough coverage." Celia made herself stop talking. She had never closed for a week. A vacation would do them both wonders—individually and as a couple—but the reality of how to make that happen was too overwhelming to think about realistically.

"Celia." Mitch said her name the way he used to—full of love and emotion. This filled her heart with hope. All was not lost.

He didn't continue, though.

"Just talk to me," she pleaded. "We can get past whatever is keeping you away." If only she had some idea of what had made Mitch walk out in the first place, then Celia would know where to start.

Mitch sighed a sigh to end all sighs. Celia stayed quiet. It was his turn to meet her halfway. "I'll think about it," he said. "I have to get to work. Bye, Celia."

"Bye."

Celia waited for Mitch to disconnect the call. It took far less time than she would have liked. Didn't he pine for her the way she did for him? Did he miss her at night? Did he regret walking out months ago?

Apparently not. He would have come back if he had any regrets.

But his 'bye' didn't sound nearly as final as when he'd left the condo with a suitcase and hadn't looked back. She'd almost lost all hope then. Now, hope was growing in her chest in waves.

Celia finished getting ready for work and biked the six miles to the bookstore. It took her less time than usual as she pedaled hard and imagined what she would say to Mitch the next time they talked. Now that the gates of communication had been opened, she wanted to make sure they didn't close again.

Inside Celia's Bookshelf, she stashed her bike and looked around at what Cori had accomplished yesterday afternoon. Everything was as it should be. Celia would miss Cori in the fall, for sure. Finding reliable high school help was difficult; Cori had broken all stereotypes Celia held against teen employees.

There was still an hour before opening, but after getting off the phone with Mitch, Celia couldn't be cooped up in the condo any longer. She started putting together tomorrow's plans for story time.

She had three piles of options when a knock on the front door interrupted her. The clock told her she'd been working for forty-five minutes, with just fifteen more to go until she unlocked the front door to customers. But this wasn't a customer knocking.

Celia opened the door and locked it once again behind her. "Hi Brooke," she said to her sister who looked like a tornado of emotion. "Sorry about last night," Celia added, assuming the anger and frustration she saw written across Brooke's face were about to be unleashed on her.

Brooke stormed past Celia into the bookstore. "I wish you'd at least texted me. Or Alice. We were both pretty disappointed. And worried."

Celia nodded. But Brooke's words didn't hold the punch Celia expected. Something else was getting to her. "I know. I should have. You're right."

Brooke turned around to face Celia. Her older sister took a breath and asked, "Is everything okay?"

Celia told her, "Mitch called yesterday as I was about to

head to Alice's."

Brooke's eyes widened and she reached behind her to grab hold of the counter. "And...?"

"And I answered. It was the first time he called in four months. What was I supposed to do?" Brooke wasn't attacking her, but Celia was still automatically on the defensive.

"I think you were supposed to answer. How did the conversation go?"

Celia told Brooke that it was quick and Mitch just wanted the papers signed, which prompted her to go to Mr. Williams's office. "That's why I missed the party. I went home to shower, and then it was just too late to make an appearance. Plus, I was too down to pretend to have fun."

Brooke nodded. "Have you talked to Alice? I think she'd understand."

"Not yet. I texted her this morning." Celia glanced to her phone. "I haven't heard back. But it's her opening day. So maybe she's busy." Brooke nodded. "And it won't be as simple as explaining last night's absence. I have to start at the beginning." Celia sighed. "I should have already told her Mitch asked for a divorce."

Tension grew between them, crackling in the air. "I might have done that yesterday," Brooke said, through clenched teeth.

Celia looked up. Before she could say anything, Brooke continued. "I'm sorry. It wasn't my place. I shouldn't have told her."

Her apology took the wind out of Celia's counterattack. "You're right, you shouldn't have said anything. But maybe that'll make it easier to tell her everything once I talk to her."

Celia unlocked the door again, officially opening Celia's

Bookshelf. She couldn't tell if Brooke was finished talking about Mitch, but she was. To change the subject, she asked, "I'm guessing you didn't come here all frazzled to talk about Mitch."

Brooke shook her head. "You're right. I didn't. I just came from Donna's office at the country club where I learned that I lost their Labor Day golf tournament contract."

The stash of coffee was running low so Celia refilled it while she listened with one ear. This story didn't seem to involve her; she still wasn't sure why Brooke was telling her.

"You want to know who did get it?" Brooke asked, the tone of her voice getting Celia to look up. "Stuart Randall," Brooke told her before she could come up with a name.

It was as if a puppeteer had pulled some strings, Celia stood up so fast. "Are you sure? I didn't even know he was putting in a bid."

Brooke's lips formed a thin line, like she was holding something back. Celia realized what.

"Of course I didn't know. Mitch would have told me if we were on speaking terms, but I don't know anything that's going on in his life right now. Don't pin this on me." Brooke's cheeks went from a light shade of pink to the deep red of sunset. "I would have warned you if I'd known. I promise."

"I'm not blaming you at all," Brooke said, but she wasn't convincing. "I just wanted to know if you knew anything."

This was a huge contract for Brooke. Without it, Celia knew her sister would be scraping smaller events together to cover the lost income. "What are you going to do?"

"I'm going to fight my way back for it. Donna said she'd pay my seventy percent of my normal fee to work with Stuart. I accepted, but I don't want that. It feels like a pity payment." There was a pause and Celia suspected she knew what was coming next. "Do you have Stuart's address?"

Celia nodded. "What are you going to tell him? Has he accepted the job?" Celia walked behind the counter to get a pen and paper.

"Not as of this morning," Brooke said, leaning against the counter. "I'm going to find out how he could afford to undercut my quote by so much. I don't see how he'll come out even at the amount he quoted. I wonder if he's planning to take a loss, hoping for a long-term contract. Donna mentioned putting me on retainer for the future, but I don't know if she has that power. If she couldn't fight the board to give me the Labor Day golf tournament, how will she manage to get me on retainer?"

Celia handed over a slip of paper with Stuart's Burlington address. She only knew it by heart because she'd had to keep herself from going there to track down Mitch. If he wanted space, she'd give him space. Within reason. And he was becoming unreasonable.

"Thanks, Celia." Brooke stuck it in her pocket and headed for the door.

"Wait!" Celia called to her before she left. "Mom called me last night. Dinner at Alice's tomorrow night?"

Brooke sighed and turned around. "They'll be back by then? Has Alice agreed?"

"Don't know." Celia shrugged. "I'm sure we'll hear more before tomorrow afternoon. Just passing on the information I have."

"I'll make sure Jared and the kids aren't busy. I think we're good, though. Thanks for the address." Brooke waved and left Celia's Bookshelf just as a customer entered.

With Brooke's departure, Celia could finish getting

tomorrow's story time books together. She settled on gardening books, even pulling some nonfiction for a display for the adults. Her customers—a couple, it seemed—browsed the shelves and tables, not appearing to have anything in particular in mind. Celia remained available but gave them plenty of space to find what they wanted.

The rest of the morning passed in similar fashion, some customers knowing exactly what they were looking for while others just window shopped. No one needed Celia's attention and she was able to balance her previous month's numbers. She'd seen a slight increase in sales over the previous month, which she often expected as the weather warmed and families dreamed about what books they would read on their summer vacations.

By early afternoon, Celia still hadn't heard back from Alice about the lunch invitation and she considered texting again. She restrained herself but was surprised when her phone rang while she was holding it.

It wasn't Alice.

"Twice in one day," Celia said, trying to sound hopeful and excited to hear from Mitch.

"Celia," Mitch said, sounding nervous. Like this was their first date, rather than almost their sixth anniversary.

"Can we talk?" Thankfully, the bookshop was empty.

"I'm outside. We can talk," Mitch said.

Now that he was ready, Celia was suddenly silent. She took a deep breath and said, "Come inside. Please."

There was a pause before Mitch responded. "Okay."

Celia disconnected the call and went to the front door. She watched her husband walk from his work truck to her bookshop. When he entered, she turned the sign on the door to *Closed* and locked the door. Mitch had her full attention.

CHAPTER TEN

Alice nearly swayed on her feet. The only Jack and Linda she'd heard of were the people who had given her life and then given her away. Were her birth parents Jack and Linda Lewis, who Mr. Thompson was here representing?

There had been plenty of times in her life, especially in her adolescence and teen years, that Alice had hated them. Whenever she felt her parents had wronged her, Alice believed she could have had a better life with Linda and Jack.

You're not my parents, she would throw at her parents when she was at her maddest.

But she'd given that game up decades ago. She'd learned that whatever had driven Jack and Linda to put her up for adoption had been too big for them to handle with a baby in their lives. She'd been given the gift of a family, and if Linda and Jack couldn't give her that, they'd done the next best thing.

Alice didn't know anything about the terms of her adoption or her adoptive parents. Her parents couldn't tell her anything. They'd assured her hundreds of times that hers had been a closed adoption. They knew nothing. And when Alice was eighteen and had done her own research to learn anything she could about her birth parents, all she'd been able to find were their first names.

The names were too common for Alice to dig any deeper on her own, and she wasn't about to hire a private investigator. She didn't have the means to do that, and something in her gut stopped her from wanting to. She'd ultimately stopped looking, realizing Jack and Linda didn't want to be found. And when she became a parent herself, it stopped mattering to her as much. She found her true self in her family.

Now it was like Linda and Jack Lewis were ghosts coming to haunt Alice.

"Come inside. We'll sit on the screened porch," Alice finally managed. She didn't know how long she left Mr. Thompson staring at her from the driveway. He seemed patient, though, not pushing her to move faster than she was comfortable.

Alice led the way inside, removing her shoes and pointing toward the screened porch with the southern view over the lake. "I'll bring water." She needed a minute before she walked down this road in her past that she thought was a dead end.

With two glasses and a pitcher of ice water on a tray, Alice walked to the screen porch with a mix of excitement and dread in her stomach. She'd wanted so much to know her birth parents thirty-five years ago. But she'd given up hope not long after.

Mr. Thompson had made himself comfortable in one of the chairs and Alice placed the tray on a table and sat on the other side of it. She filled a glass for herself and took a sip. It wasn't too hot yet, being only early June, but the ice water helped tame her anticipation.

"I have some papers to go over with you," Mr. Thompson started. He reached into his briefcase and pulled out a thick folder.

Alice suddenly realized why Mr. Thompson was here. She'd thought that perhaps Linda and Jack wanted to meet her and they'd sent their lawyer to test the waters.

No. That wasn't the case. He was a probate lawyer, here to settle Jack and Linda's estate.

If Alice was going to ever meet her birth parents, her chance had passed.

Mr. Thompson opened the folder and her suspicions were confirmed.

The first thought Alice had was not that she missed ever meeting her birth parents, but that she had done this exact thing six months ago when Peter passed. She'd managed to get everything settled far more quickly than usual since they'd had fair warning that he was dying. It had not come as a surprise and everything had already been lined up, their lawyer just waiting for the call.

That hadn't made the process any easier on Alice and the girls, but she'd been given access to capital to purchase the inn far more quickly than she'd expected.

"They're dead, aren't they?" Alice asked, rather coldly she realized after the words had left her mouth.

Mr. Thompson looked up, his fingers no longer rifling through the pages. "Yes. I... I thought you knew."

Alice shook her head. "Of course you did. You didn't know the details of our relationship, I suppose."

The lawyer leaned back in his chair, apparently waiting for Alice to explain.

"I never met them," she told him. He nodded once,

slowly, digesting that information. "So anything you have to share about them would be greatly appreciated."

His hands came to a rest on his belly. "I can only share what's in these folders, I'm afraid," he told her.

Alice nodded, ready to move forward. If she was going to learn who her birth parents were, this was a start. Perhaps she'd have enough information to dig deeper after today.

If she wanted to.

Mr. Thompson found the paper he was looking for and handed it across to Alice. On it, the broad overview of the Lewis' estate was outlined. Alice was the sole heir.

"They had no children," he told her. "Other than you. They wanted everything to go to you."

It was Alice's turn to lean back in her chair to digest this news. Just as with Peter's will, everything came to Alice. But that had not been a surprise. She was his wife of twenty-five years. They'd had a life together.

Receiving everything from two people she'd never met knocked the wind out of Alice.

Jack and Linda had given her life. Now they were giving her everything they had at the time of their deaths.

"How did they die?" she asked in a whisper.

Mr. Thompson cleared his throat. Without a word, he picked up a newspaper article and handed it to Alice. It had been cut out so she couldn't see what newspaper it had come from, but there was a date written in pen across the top. The article had been published two months earlier. Her birth parents had died two months ago and she hadn't felt a thing. She'd always thought that even though she didn't know them, she'd feel some connection to them.

Instead, nothing.

Alice scanned the short article, learning that Linda and

Jack had been on board a small private airplane with three others. It had gone down, leaving no survivors.

There was nothing for Alice to say. She let Mr. Thompson deliver the rest of the details about the estate she was set to inherit while she held onto the small newspaper article for dear life. This would be the closest she'd come to ever talking to the people who had brought her into this world.

In the end, she would receive a healthy financial sum and the proceeds from the sale of their house in southern Vermont. She was free to come and claim anything that was in the house, or sell all of their belongings how she saw fit. Alternatively, Mr. Thompson could handle all of that for her, which was the route Alice agreed to.

For years—maybe her whole life—Alice had lived in the same state as Jack and Linda and she'd never met them. Never even known they existed.

When Mr. Thompson finished with the legalities, he passed Alice an envelope. It was blank on the outside. And sealed. She looked at the lawyer curiously but he just smiled.

"Unless you have any questions, I'll see myself out," he said, handing her his card. "I'll be in touch in the next week."

Alice nodded and watched him go. She turned the envelope over again, then slid her finger beneath the seal. It came apart easily, like the glue had dried over time or it had never been sealed properly.

There was a single sheet of paper inside that Alice unfolded. The first thing she noted was the date from twelve years ago. This was not a new letter, but had probably been written whenever the estate had last been updated.

The handwriting reminded her of her grandmother's—sloping cursive that she had to take her time to decipher. Condensation collected on her water glass as Alice read the first and last words she would ever read from her birth parents.

Dear Alice,

There is no explanation that a daughter can accept for her parents' choice to give her up for adoption. I know. I was also adopted.

I'm sorry that Jack and I never met you, even though you sought us out years ago. You left your contact information, though we only recently learned that. Because of that, though, we were able to make you the sole beneficiary to our estate. It's the least we can do.

Please know that we have thought of you daily and hoped that you lived the best life possible. We had always wanted a child but had given up that dream by the time I became pregnant. We were overjoyed!

Then, things that were out of our control made it clear that we would be unable to give you the life you deserved. I will not make excuses. It was the hardest decision of our lives to choose to give you away. Our greatest hope is that you've had a loving family that provided you with happiness and joy.

There were also plenty of times that Jack or I wanted to reach out and find you. We wanted you to know where you'd come from and to make sense of our choice. But we also knew that if we met you, we would have too many regrets. Perhaps that was selfish, perhaps not. That is for you to decide.

I know that anything you receive at the time of our deaths will pale in comparison to what a relationship can provide, but please accept it with an open heart. We give you all our love.

Linda and Jack Lewis

Alice read the letter twice before she felt anything.

Jack and Linda had found her but chose to keep their distance.

Time seemed to stop as Alice thought about everything she'd just learned. It was like she'd turned a page in the story of her life but there was a whole chapter missing. She was lost, when at one time in her life learning even the last names of her birth parents would have helped her find her identity.

But that was decades ago when Alice was still a teen, searching and trying on different identities. Now, at forty-nine years old with two grown children and a deceased husband, Alice knew exactly who she was. She didn't need others to define her. She could do that herself.

Alice reached for her glass of ice water, only to find that the ice had melted. She took a sip anyway, hardly refreshed.

At eighteen, Alice had contacted the adoption agency her parents had provided her with, and even the state, looking anywhere for a path toward her birth parents. She'd been met with roadblock after roadblock. Jack and Linda had not left any information that would be available to Alice, so she left her own contact information—her name, date of birth, home address and phone number. While those had changed over the years, it would have been easy for Jack and Linda to find her.

And they had.

But not for the reason Alice had hoped for. She wanted to know them. Now that she knew they'd found her, there was a hole in her heart where their love should have been.

Alice tried to put herself in their shoes. Something had happened in their lives that had made them unable to raise a child. But they'd still given her life. Would Alice have been able to do the same? She didn't think so. Holding both Viv and Nora for the first time had melted Alice's heart. She never could have turned her backs on them.

But she also didn't have to. She had a supportive husband and family. They were financially stable with a comfortable home, enough to eat, and a loving community. If she had found herself without any of those supports, maybe she could have done the unimaginable—asked strangers to give her child what she couldn't. A loving home.

She shook her head, coming back to the present, thankful for all that she had. Alice stood and brought the tray back inside. It was now early afternoon and Alice found her unmade lunch on the counter. Her stomach growled at the sight. She ate standing up and checked her phone for messages.

There was nothing on her business line. She looked at her cell phone and saw a missed text from Celia. It had come in several hours ago.

Sorry I missed last night's party. Come to lunch at the bookstore and I'll explain? Alice read. Last night felt like ancient history suddenly. Mr. Thompson's bombshell announcements —both of who her birth parents were, and that she was receiving another inheritance—had flipped her world over. Whatever had kept Celia away last night no longer mattered.

Celia was her sister. Her family. And that was stronger than any glue.

Missed lunch and have guests arriving. Will try to stop by before their arrival but might have to wait until another time, Alice responded. She wanted to be there for her sister but, no matter how hard she tried, she couldn't be in two places at once. Being at the North Star Inn was her priority right now.

Alice finished her small lunch, then turned to another item on her mental checklist: calling her daughters for tomorrow's family dinner. Viv was first because Alice wanted to get her older daughter to open up about her relationship with Aiden.

Another piece of information that seemed old already, though she'd just learned it this morning.

"Hi Mom. You caught me on my lunch break. What's up? Do you have your first guests?" Viv asked as soon as she answered.

Alice was a little taken aback by the onslaught of questions. "I'm glad I caught you, then. No guests yet but they should be here soon. I won't keep you if you're on your lunch break. I was calling about tomorrow night—"

"What's tomorrow night?" Viv asked, sounding worried, like she'd forgotten something.

"Grandma and Grandpa are heading home and they asked for a family dinner at the Inn tomorrow night. Are you free?"

"Hang on." Alice knew that both of her daughters kept digital calendars. She hadn't made the change herself, preferring to write things down with a pen. But Viv and Nora had everything in their phones. "I'll be there," Viv said.

"Great." She paused, considering how to broach the subject of Aiden. "I saw Hope at the farmer's market this morning. She said to tell you hello," Alice said, hoping Viv would take the bait.

"I haven't seen her in a while. How's she doing?" The bait was not taken.

"Good." Alice had promised to keep Hope's news of Viv and Aiden's relationship a secret so she didn't add anything else. "I'll let you get back to lunch, then. See you tomorrow night."

"Okay. Bye, Mom."

Alice hung up just as she heard tires crunching the gravel in the driveway. She quickly put her dishes in the dishwasher and went to the front door. An elderly couple was getting out of their car with New York license plates.

"Welcome to the North Star Inn," Alice said as she walked to their car to help with their bags.

Her first guests had arrived. She was open for business.

CHAPTER ELEVEN

Brooke walked out of Celia's Bookshelf as calmly as she could. She'd entered with a boatload of frustration, and she hadn't exactly burned any off. At least she knew what happened last night to keep Celia away from Alice's launch party. But she still had Stuart stealing her biggest client to deal with.

As she walked down the street to her car—the nearest parking spot she'd been able to find was two blocks away—she continued fuming about Donna blaming everything on the country club's board. Donna had to have had at least some weight.

Once in her car, Brooke sat with the engine off for several minutes. What was she going to say to Stuart once she found him? All she had was his home address. Was she taking this too far? Would she be able to keep everything strictly professional once Mitch's brother was in front of her?

What if Mitch was there? Celia hadn't seen him in four months and now Brooke was headed to the very home where he was staying.

Stuart winning the country club's event contract was not Mitch's fault. It just felt like Mitch leaving Celia with a broken heart and Stuart underbidding Brooke were two slaps in the face too many. They weren't connected. They just happened to be brothers, and Celia and Brooke happened to be sisters. Of course their lives would be interconnected.

But mixing personal and business lives was never a good idea.

Brooke took a deep breath and started her car. She would drive to the address Celia had given her and take it from there. Maybe she wouldn't even knock. Maybe.

The music coming through the car's speakers was suddenly interrupted with a call over Brooke's Bluetooth.

"Brooke Hastings," she said after she used her thumb on the steering wheel to answer. She couldn't afford not to answer a call. Anyone could be a potential client right now.

"Hi Brooke. This is Amy at Growing Daisies."

"Is everything okay?" Brooke asked before Amy could say anything else. After last night's scare with Tina, Brooke immediately imagined a dozen scenarios of Emma getting hurt on her preschool's playground.

"Everything's fine. Emma's fine. But it seems that she forgot her stuffed elephant and she's very upset about it. If you have a chance, could you bring it by? And if you can't, that's fine, too."

Brooke sighed and looked in the backseat when she stopped at a light. There was Tiger, Emma's ridiculously named stuffed elephant. She knew that there would be no quiet time for Emma without Tiger.

"I can bring it by. Thanks for calling, Amy," Brooke said, then hung up.

Stuart would have to wait. If she hadn't been distracted

this morning with preparing her argument for Donna, maybe she wouldn't have missed reminding Emma to grab Tiger.

Excuses would get her nowhere, though. Brooke took a deep breath and let it all go. She was a good mom—a great mom. Everyone made mistakes. Even Jared, who did far more drop-offs than Brooke.

Keeping Emma happy at preschool was more important than finding Stuart at home. She could always find his office if needed. Emma went to preschool every weekday, and the fewer morning meltdowns she had, the better.

Unfortunately, Growing Daisies was on the northern end of Golden Bay and Brooke was heading to Burlington, a half hour south. She turned around, knowing that this side trip would add almost a half hour to her morning.

Oh well. Her kids were worth it.

Amy was relieved when Brooke dropped Tiger off in her office, and Brooke was pretty sure it wouldn't have been okay if she hadn't made time to swing by with the beloved elephant. Brooke snuck back out to her car before Emma could spot her.

Then it was back to business. She plugged Stuart's home address into her phone's GPS and headed south. It was nearing noon and she was skeptical that he would even be home at this point. If he worked for a national corporation, then they probably paid for him to have an office—unlike Brooke, who'd made a corner of their basement into her home office.

As Brooke drove, the silence of the car calmed her. Reason started to take hold in her mind. Mitch and Celia's marital troubles were not connected to Brooke and Stuart's business competition. If Mitch and Celia weren't in the midst of a possible divorce, Stuart would still want the country club contract. What event planner in the greater Burlington area wouldn't?

The address was difficult to find with one-way streets throwing a curveball. But Brooke eventually found the house in a quiet part of the Queen City. She parked and walked up to the front door. A woman opened the door almost as soon as she knocked.

"Hello. I'm looking for Stuart Randall," Brooke said as friendly as she could muster.

"Sorry. He's not in." The woman offered her a sympathetic smile. "Are you a client?"

Brooke considered using that opening, but she was above lying to get what she wanted. She shook her head. "Brooke Hastings. I guess you'd say I'm healthy competition."

"Well, if it's work related, I can give you his office address. He's just around the block."

The woman—who Brooke assumed was Stuart's wife, though Celia had never mentioned a wedding for Mitch's brother, at least not that Brooke remembered—left the door open as she walked back into the middle of the house. Brooke took that as a friendly invitation to step inside.

"Here," she said, returning to the front door which Brooke had left cracked behind her. Brooke took the offered paper with the address on it and thanked her before leaving.

Rather than drive around on one-way streets and hope for another convenient parking space, Brooke walked to the address of Stuart's office. She let herself inside the building and found Stuart's office with no trouble. She knocked on his open door and he looked up from behind his computer. His resemblance to Mitch was always surprising, even if they were brothers.

"Good morning," he said.

"Brooke Hastings," Brooke said, extending her hand in his direction.

There was only a moment of surprised recognition that crossed his face before he quickly hid it. "What can I do for you?" he asked. "You're not here to talk about Mitch and Celia, are you?"

Brooke chuckled. "No. But anything you told me about that situation would be passed on to Celia, just so you know."

"Fair enough," Stuart said with a grin. "What can I do for you, then?" He motioned to a chair across the desk from him and Brooke sat.

"I talked to Donna this morning." Brooke didn't elaborate right away, waiting for Stuart to react. He didn't. "At the Golden Bay Country Club."

Stuart nodded.

"It seems we'll be working together for the Labor Day golf tournament," Brooke added.

Stuart nodded again. There was no joy in his expression. "I just received her email a little while ago. I was looking over the contract when you came in."

Brooke had to admit that she was less than thrilled to have to work with Stuart for the event in order to stay in the country club's good graces for future events, but Stuart's ice-cold attitude was not exactly going to make it any easier to mix their services.

"And?" Brooke asked, hoping to move this conversation forward.

"And I was very surprised to receive the contract."

Brooke was surprised, and it must have shown on her face, because Stuart continued, "I thought I'd bid high."

At this, Brooke accidentally let a laugh escape. She

shouldn't have known what he'd quoted the country club, but Donna told her this morning.

"You know, don't you?" he asked.

Brooke nodded. "Not the exact number, but ballpark."

"Well, then I should tell you that I won't be accepting. You know as well as I do that the number I gave them is totally undoable."

Brooke's heart jumped into her throat. He wasn't going to accept the job? Hope and surprise mixed, probably making her look stunned.

"I transposed two numbers in the quote," Stuart admitted.

Brooke's mouth fell open even further. "You're kidding."

Stuart shook his head. "I couldn't believe it this morning when I saw the contract from Donna with the price they'd agreed to. Then I checked it with my original proposal, and the numbers matched." Stuart threw his hands in the air. "I guess I got sloppy. I can't accept at that price, and to maintain my own professional integrity, I'm simply refusing the job."

Brooke was stunned into speechlessness.

"It'll be yours," Stuart told her. "If you still want it."

Brooke shook the surprise from her mind and smiled. "Yes. I'll wait to hear from Donna for confirmation, though."

Stuart nodded. "Of course. I understand that you've been their go-to event planner for some time now. It must have come as a shock when you didn't get the contract."

This was not at all how Brooke had imagined this conversation going. She'd been prepared to fight him at every turn, even with her personal feelings about his brother pushed aside. The wind had been taken right out of her sails, and it must have shown.

"If you ever expand into Burlington events, give me a call," Stuart said, handing Brooke a card. "And I'll stay out of your territory in Golden Bay."

Brooke took the card, still epically surprised at the way this meeting had unfolded. She stood to leave, but turned back to Stuart.

"Before I go, how's Mitch? I'm sure Celia would like at least that much information."

Stuart shrugged, still standing behind his desk. "Haven't seen him in weeks. Last I knew, he was waiting on the papers from Celia. But as far as I could tell, he didn't really want the divorce. He just feels like that's the only way forward."

Brooke was stunned once again. She managed to clear her mind for one final question. "Why?"

Stuart shook his head. "It's not my place to say. I hope he'll talk to Celia before they do something they'll regret."

Brooke finally left Stuart's office, hope growing in her chest—for her business's future, and for her sister's marriage.

From the little bit that Stuart revealed, one major question had surfaced. If Stuart hadn't seen Mitch for weeks, where was he staying?

CHAPTER TWELVE

With Mitch in front of Celia for the first time in four months, Celia suddenly didn't know what to say. She'd spent months wishing for exactly this—the two of them alone, together. The conversations she needed to have with him had played out in her mind at all hours of the days —in the shower, awake in the middle of the night, over reheated leftover dinners, biking to and from work. She had never been at a loss for words when she was alone and imagining a conversation with her husband.

Reality told a different story.

Celia motioned her hand toward two reading chairs between stacks of books. Mitch took a seat, as did Celia. She remained silent.

"How have you been?" Mitch asked.

His simple question released the floodgates. Tears immediately sprang to Celia's eyes as she relived the last four months in an instant. Mitch packing a suitcase, not hearing from him, receiving the divorce papers, even meeting with Mr. Williams last night.

"I'm so sorry," Mitch said. "I didn't want to hurt you."

Mitch's words did not match his actions. And he seemed to realize that. There was such tenderness in his words that Celia knew he still had feelings for her. Had he only been staying away to hide those feelings? "I didn't know what else to do."

Celia finally found her voice. "Why?" she asked him. That was the only thing she needed an answer to, though he could interpret it a million different ways.

Why did you leave?

Why didn't you call?

Why was there no other option?

Why didn't you come back?

Why did you stay away?

Why didn't you know what else to do?

Why was leaving ever a possible solution?

Rather than answering any of her unasked questions with words, Mitch slid a photo across the table.

Celia took it between her fingers and studied the boy in the picture. He looked like Mitch as a child. Why was he showing her this?

"What is this?" Celia asked. "Who is this?"

Mitch took a deep breath and looked at the photo, rather than at Celia, while he answered. "That's Dylan. He's twelve-years-old. And he's... my son."

Mitch's words couldn't seem to penetrate Celia's reality. The boy's name was Dylan and he was twelve. She could make sense of that. But Mitch's son? Mitch didn't have a son.

Celia looked from the boy in the photo to Mitch. There was no denying that there was a striking resemblance between the two. But Mitch had a son? Celia couldn't wrap her mind around that statement. There must be some mistake.

"He's your... son?" Celia asked, trying out the word.

Their eyes met for the first time since the bomb was dropped and Celia saw pain she didn't expect.

"I didn't know what to do," he said, not really explaining any of the questions swirling around Celia's mind.

"When...?" Celia asked, unable to form the rest of her question right away. She swallowed and tried again, holding Mitch's kind gaze. "When did you find out?"

"January twenty-eighth."

At the time, Celia hadn't known about Dylan, but she knew what happened barely a week later. Mitch had suddenly packed a suitcase and left.

"Why didn't you tell me?" Celia whispered. "Why did you let Dylan break us apart?"

Mitch sighed and looked back at the photo. She could see that he was trying.

"You know I never wanted to be a father. And you accepted that when we started dating and then married. Parenthood just wasn't something I could see myself doing. When I got the letter from Lisa—Dylan's mom—with this photo, I knew she wasn't lying. But I couldn't believe it."

Mitch's hands twisted around themselves in his lap and Celia leaned forward to calm them. She placed one hand on his. Her touch seemed to bring him back to the present.

"Lisa was your girlfriend before we met, right?" Celia asked, knowing the answer but having to say something.

Mitch nodded.

Celia released Mitch's hands and leaned back. She'd worried for a moment that Dylan had been the product of an affair early in their relationship, but if he was twelve and Lisa was his mother, that was impossible. The last Celia had heard about Lisa, she had moved to California. She didn't know if the woman was still there, but Dylan's age spoke for itself. Dylan was born before Celia had ever met Mitch. He had done nothing wrong.

Mitch stood and ran his hand through his hair. Celia knew more was coming but she wasn't going to press him. She'd waited this long; she could wait another moment. He took a deep breath and continued.

"You can see that Dylan looks just like me. But I requested a paternity test. I'd always been so careful. Even in my early twenties, I knew I didn't want to accidentally fall into fatherhood."

Mitch started pacing while Celia stayed seated. She didn't have the strength to stand.

With his back to her, Mitch continued. "She agreed and got the test. I got the results two months ago. Then I filed for divorce."

Mitch's voice cracked. "I'm so sorry, Celia," he said, tearing up.

Celia finally stood and walked toward Mitch. He turned and met her halfway. She remained silent, waiting for more.

"I didn't know what to do. You'd changed your mind and wanted kids. I still didn't. And suddenly I was a father. It felt like a slap in your face that I couldn't do to you."

Celia was stunned. "Divorce seemed like the better option," she said, at least trying to understand where he was coming from, even if she didn't agree with him.

Mitch nodded sadly.

Celia reached a hand out and touched Mitch's arm. He didn't react, but he didn't recoil, either. She dared to go further by taking a step toward him. "Mitch, we can get past anything as long as we are on the same team. But I haven't felt like we're on the same team for a while now."

She took another step toward her husband, hoping that he would make the next move.

He remained immobile. They were nearly standing on top of each other by now. She could sense the uncertainty emanating from his body. Without thinking about it, she reached her arms around his neck and let her head fall to his chest.

Thankfully, Mitch raised his arms and embraced her.

"I just didn't want to hurt you. Dylan is my son," Mitch whispered. "I didn't mean to do this to you. But I had to do right by him."

Celia let the silence fill the space around them. Tears stung her eyes as she realized what a devoted father Mitch was. For something he'd never wanted and was suddenly thrown into, he seemed to know the right thing to do. If at her expense.

"You were so disappointed that I didn't want to become a father with you," Mitch continued. "I just couldn't—"

Celia leaned back in Mitch's arm and placed a finger on Mitch's lips. "You couldn't, but now you did. We can get past this. I'm not going to sign those papers," she whispered.

Mitch nodded, Celia's finger still against his mouth.

"I may want to be a mother," Celia admitted, "but I want to be your wife more. Parenthood is a huge commitment, and if you don't want a baby with me, I respect that. I don't take it personally. We can love Dylan together."

Celia removed her finger and stepped back. Mitch held on with both hands, keeping her within reach.

"Dylan is twelve. He was born before you ever met me. There is no shame in having relationships before we met. And whatever happened in them, happened. Dylan is lucky to have you as a father, now that he knows about you." Celia had a sudden thought. "He does know about you, doesn't he?"

Mitch smiled. "Yes. Lisa and Dylan moved back to Vermont a couple years ago. They don't live in Golden Bay, but I've visited them a couple times in the last few months."

Celia saw him put the brakes on before he said anything else. They'd spent the last four months apart and she knew nothing of what he'd been up to.

"Tell me about him," Celia said, taking Mitch's hand and leading him back to the chairs.

She felt that they'd turned a corner in this conversation and in their relationship. The divorce had barely been mentioned. She had hope that they could move forward. Together.

Mitch smiled and Celia's heart grew for him. He held the photo back up to look at it before he began.

"He's on the middle school basketball team. Or was, in the winter. It's his favorite sport." Mitch chuckled. "It's kind of ironic, because he's pretty short still. I was a late bloomer when it came to the adolescent growth spurt, and Dylan might be the same."

Celia saw love in Mitch's eyes. She thought again how great of a father he was going to be. It seemed to come naturally.

"He's also in the band. He plays the trumpet. Lisa told me he loves it and practices every day. She wants to soundproof his bedroom."

Dylan sounded like a great kid—a variety of interests with dedication to learning and improving.

"And he loves roller coasters," Mitch said, looking up with a huge grin on his face. "Lisa hates them. She won't go on them. She's taken him to amusement parks a couple times and she makes sure to always bring one of his friends so she doesn't have to ride the roller coasters with him."

Celia matched Mitch's smile.

"I've never told you this, Celia, but when I met you ten years ago on our first date, within five minutes I had this feeling... this feeling that I was looking at my wife. I know it sounds crazy, but I just... knew."

Celia hadn't felt the same clarity on their first date, but there had been an intensity she'd never felt before. An intensity she hadn't wanted to let go. And she didn't want to let that go now, either.

When Mitch had shown up at the bookstore barely an hour ago, Celia hadn't known what to expect. All she'd known was that he was finally willing to talk to her. She didn't know what he would say and if it would end their marriage.

Dylan was not going to end their marriage.

But she did have a concern that must be voiced.

"It sounds like he's a really good kid," Celia said as Mitch beamed at her.

"But...?" Mitch asked. "It sounds like a but is coming."

Celia grinned and looked down at her lap. It was her turn to be at a loss for words. But she wasn't going to take four months to say something. "What concerns me is not that Dylan exists—he's an exciting new chapter in our lives if you're willing to rejoin me. But," she drew out the word dramatically, "I'm worried that you felt you couldn't say anything to me. I'm hurt that you felt you had to keep Dylan a secret when really you'd done nothing wrong."

Mitch nodded. "I know. I didn't mean to keep Dylan a secret. You have to believe me that I meant to tell you in February. Even in January. But then as each day passed, it felt harder and harder to go back and tell you the truth."

Celia waited again for more. She took a lesson from Alice's book and kept her mouth shut.

"Filing for divorce was a mistake," he said. "I hope that you'll forgive that. I've missed you every single day I've been away. I don't want to be away anymore."

Celia was relieved. She could live with that apology for now. They had a future together. They could work to be better. Better together.

"Let's get your stuff from Stuart's," she said. "Cori should be here any minute and I can help you. I want you to come back home."

The love that had been coming from Mitch's gaze suddenly grew cold. He looked away, unable to meet her eye anymore.

"What?" Celia asked. "Don't do this again. Don't hold something back."

Mitch smiled. "You're right. There is something else I have to tell you, though."

Celia wasn't sure she was ready for another bombshell. All the hope she'd been feeling suddenly seemed like it could vanish in an instant.

"I haven't been staying with Stuart."

CHAPTER THIRTEEN

Alice took hold of the largest suitcase while David Munroe took the smaller. Stella was left with just her handbag.

"I hope that you'll have a relaxing weekend here," Alice said as she led the way inside, pushing aside all thoughts of her birth parents' gift.

"I have four rooms, though only two of them will be occupied this weekend. You're here in Lyra," Alice said, when they reached the guest rooms below the screened porch. Having the Inn built into the side of a hill offered extra privacy for her guest rooms. They entered on the main floor, then went down to the bedrooms that were not visible from the street. Views of the lake were easy to come by from anywhere on the south side of the building.

"It looks perfect," Stella said.

"This isn't named after the constellation Lyra, is it?" David asked.

Alice smiled. She suspected that not many guests would guess how she picked her rooms' names—Lyra, Aquarius, Orion, and Virgo. Some sounded like Zodiac signs associated with one's date of birth. But Alice and Peter had chosen them as seasonal constellations they particularly liked.

Alice had known nothing about astronomy when she'd met Peter, who had made learning constellations somewhat of an obsessive hobby. She'd quickly learned that he was the worst at remembering the meaning and myth behind each constellation after he read the history once. So they'd made up their own myths. They had become a running joke among the family, and it felt only appropriate that she kept that humor and passion alive at the Inn.

"It is named for the constellation," Alice said, leaving the heavy suitcase in the bedroom. "My husband and I would try to catch the Lyrid meteor shower every spring. The weather didn't always agree, but we tried our best when the sky wasn't covered in a blanket of clouds."

David nodded his appreciation. "He was a professor of astronomy in his former life," Stella spoke up.

Alice was dumbfounded. Her first guests, and the perfection of the rooms' names was already coming to fruition. "Well, if I have any questions while you're here, I'll pick your brain about it. For now, though, I'll let you get settled. Come up whenever you're ready and I'll have tea and a snack on the screened porch."

The Munroes appeared to be easy first guests, appreciating even the small things about the Inn, and that settled some of Alice's nerves. She didn't think she'd be this nervous if it hadn't been for Mr. Thompson's surprise appearance just before their arrival. The news of her inheritance and learning about Linda and Jack Lewis weighed heavily on her mind as she returned to the kitchen to prepare an afternoon treat.

Alice filled a tray with three mugs and plates, slices of

blueberry cake that Heather had snuck into her bag with her bread purchases this morning, a pot of hot water and a smattering of tea bags, and the welcome packet that she had meticulously crafted to answer any possible question that may arise. Alice would of course be available for anything that couldn't be found in the packet, but she wanted her guests to feel a sense of independence while they enjoyed a quiet visit.

Alice left the tray in the kitchen and headed out to the porch with a book. Instead of opening it, though, she made herself comfortable and looked out to the water. Ever since Alice was little, she'd found solace on the shores of Lake Champlain. Whether it was collecting rocks along the shore, building sand castles, or walking through a wooded section, Alice felt at home with the sound of the water and birds.

Today was no different. She might not be down at the shore, but the lake offered her the same comfort.

Rather than stew in her thoughts of the past and what might have been—both with her birth parents and with Peter—Alice took out her cell phone to call Nora about tomorrow night's family dinner. Nora answered on the first ring.

"Hi Mom," she said, sounding cheery.

"Hi Nora." Alice didn't call her youngest daughter often, usually waiting for Nora to call her instead. Nora seemed to live life at full speed and was hard to catch. "I wasn't sure you'd be able to answer."

"Oh. I was just getting outside for a quick walk. There was some drama between some colleagues and I had to get away from it."

Alice smiled. She was once again thankful that she worked alone. "Is everything okay?"

"Oh yeah. It'll be fine. It had nothing to do with me but I didn't want to be there for the fallout." Nora paused for a moment but Alice could hear her breathing hard. She must have been walking fast to work out her frustration. "Is everything okay with you? I didn't expect to hear from you today with your first guests arriving."

Alice was thankful she had such thoughtful and caring daughters. "Everything's great. My first guests are here getting settled and I'm expecting another couple any time. But I wanted to catch you in between because Grandma and Grandpa are coming home tomorrow and want to see everyone. Are you available for dinner at the Inn?"

"Of course! I can't wait! I'm so glad they got the RV fixed!" Nora's enthusiasm for the return of her grandparents was contagious and Alice started to feel more excitement for the dinner she didn't really want.

"They said to plan for five, but they'll be driving most of the day so it could be earlier or later. Come any time." Alice didn't know when anyone else would show up, everyone having such different schedules—Brooke with young kids, Celia with the bookstore busiest on the weekends, Alice with guests to be available for, and Viv and Nora in their early twenties and living life to the fullest. She knew her daughters packed their weekends full, having only two days to see friends, do activities outside, and enjoy the beauty of the area.

"Is it okay if I come early and just head down to the beach?"

"Of course! Come for lunch if you'd like." Alice would love to have her girls around more. It warmed her heart that they wanted to be around, too.

Alice heard another car in the driveway and she knew she had to get off the phone. "I think my other guests just arrived. I'll see you tomorrow. Text before you come if you like. But I should be here."

"Bye, Mom. See you tomorrow." Nora hung up and Alice stood. She headed back out front and found another car, just as she suspected she would.

"Welcome to the North Star Inn," she said once she was outside.

A young couple had exited the car and the man was collecting bags from the trunk of their sedan. Alice only knew that Astrid and Karl were celebrating their honeymoon and would be spending a weekend at the Inn before heading across the Atlantic, she couldn't remember where to. She looked forward to having young love under her roof.

The young woman waved, a smile filled with joy on her face. "You must be Alice."

"Guilty. Can I help you with bags?" she asked.

Karl handed her a small bag but kept the largest for himself. "Thank you. We're so excited to be here," he said.

"Let me show you to your room where you can get settled."

Alice noticed that the smile on Astrid's face didn't waver for even a moment. This couple was so clearly in love and excited to have taken the step of marriage. Alice was happy for them, and happy that they'd selected her Inn for the first stop on their honeymoon.

She'd planned appropriately.

"I've put you here, in Virgo," she said, holding open the door to their bedroom.

"Like the horoscope?" Astrid asked.

This was the answer Alice expected. "Like the constellation, actually. I've made it the honeymoon suite."

Karl and Astrid exchanged a guilty look. "Because Virgo

means virgin in Latin?" Karl asked, a mix of worry and guilt in his eyes.

Alice laughed a deep belly laugh. She had completely overlooked that misunderstanding. Maybe she'd have to change the name. "Oh, no," she sputtered between laughter. She placed the bag on the bed and explained. "Spica is one of the brightest stars in the sky and is in the constellation, Virgo. It's actually two stars orbiting each other and causing them to be slightly not spherical. My husband and I could never remember the myths that went with the constellations, so we made up our own. And for Spica, we said that the two stars were star-crossed lovers destined to remain apart but were constantly drawn to each other. Their love shined brightest on the darkest nights."

Astrid's hand went to her heart. "I love that story. It's probably better than whatever the real story was."

"I'm not sure about that because I don't remember what the true story of Virgo is." Alice stood and added, "I'll let you two get settled. I have another couple who may be ready for tea. When you're ready, come upstairs to the screened porch for tea and we'll go over any last-minute details."

"Thanks again," Karl said, and Alice left them alone.

By now, the hot water Alice had prepared had cooled, so she heated it again. She filled a second tray and left it in the kitchen for when Astrid and Karl were ready to finalize their payments.

Alice returned to the same chair on the porch and placed the tray of tea and snacks for David and Stella on the table, her book abandoned next to it.

Before she knew it, Alice heard the porch door open and she turned to see Stella and David looking out at the view with the same awe Alice felt.

"You've got quite the spot, here," Stella admitted. "It's stunning."

Alice motioned to the couch along the wall of the Inn for Stella and David to sit. "I agree. I'll never get tired of the sights and sounds."

Alice placed mugs and plates in front of her guests, then took one for herself. Stella chose vanilla tea while David went for black. Alice chose peppermint for herself.

"Should you have any questions during your stay, this folder is full of answers." Alice placed the folder on the table near her guests for them to peruse at their leisure. "There are local activities listed, as well as dining options. I'll provide breakfast, of course, but there are some spectacular restaurants for lunch and dinner in Golden Bay and further out if you want to travel a bit. Burlington is only a half hour south."

Stella sipped her tea and winced. Maybe Alice shouldn't have reheated the water. She didn't need anyone burned on Day One.

"Do you have any phone chargers?" David asked. "We seem to have forgotten ours."

"In fact, I do. What kind of phone?"

"Samsung," David told her, holding up his phone as proof.

Alice left her guests alone on the porch to enjoy their afternoon tea and cake. She said a silent thanks to Viv, who had foreseen this exact scenario. Alice had been ready to toss all the cords she'd acquired over the years when she was moving out of her home and into the Inn. Viv had convinced her otherwise, even helping her organize them by connection type so she could provide extra charging cables to her forgetful guests.

Alice returned minutes later with the cord in hand. "Here you go," she said, handing it to David.

"Thank you." He put it on the table next to their welcome folder.

"This bread is delicious," Stella gushed, mopping up the crumbs on her plate and licking her finger with a guilty expression. "Did you make it?"

Alice shook her head. She'd planned to make something but the day had gotten away from her. Thankfully, Heather had her covered. "A baker friend did. You'll have some of her bread tomorrow morning for breakfast, too. And can buy some to bring home from the farmer's market tomorrow morning if you're interested."

"I can't wait," Stella said, leaning back and picking up her tea again. This time, the tea didn't seem to burn her lips.

"Do you have any specific plans for this weekend?" Alice asked as she leaned back and sipped her own tea. She felt like she was talking to her grandparents. Stella and David were easy company, exuding calm and an enjoyment of everything life had to offer.

The elderly couple exchanged a look that contained decades' worth of love. That single expression sent Alice's heart fluttering. She'd seen it before from Peter and knew that she'd also given the same loving look to her late husband.

"We're celebrating our anniversary," Stella said, a smile lighting up her face. "Fifty years."

Alice wasn't surprised after seeing the love they shared. "Congratulations! What a special time. The Inn is just filled with love this weekend. The other guests are newlyweds."

"I thought that might be the case," Stella admitted. She seemed to be the talker in the couple, much like Peter used to be for Alice. "I heard them giggling their way around their room. Such young love."

"We were actually supposed to be married in this very building fifty years ago," David supplied. "That's why we chose it for this weekend. We were surprised to see that it was under new ownership."

Alice put her tea down for this story. "You were supposed to be married here? What happened? Why weren't you?"

Stella crossed her legs and leaned forward. "We were weeks away from getting married, and everything was in place." Stella obviously loved telling this story. "Our parents wouldn't let us spend the night with each other, times were different back then. And we couldn't wait to get married to be together all the time." A look of wistfulness came over her face. "We thought we'd have to wait when we heard about the fire. It was ruled as arson. We couldn't get our money back because there was nothing left to give. We ended up getting married in court, and it was still the best day of our lives."

Alice was stunned. She hadn't researched back that far when she'd bought the Inn. It had needed plenty of work when she became the owner, but there was no longer any evidence of a fire.

"I had no idea," Alice said. "What happened with the Inn after?"

"Well, the owners had to sell because they had no means to fix it back up. They lost everything. They were younger than you at the time, but they had to start over from scratch. I don't know what happened to them. I remember the woman was pregnant, and I kept putting myself in her shoes. Even as a young bride, I wanted a family. But I knew it wouldn't be easy. To be pregnant with no home and no business? I still can't imagine."

Stella shook her head.

"The building sat for years," David added. "I think it finally sold for pennies and whoever bought it had to gut it to rebuild." He looked around at the screened porch, taking in Alice's more recent updates. "You've changed it since then, I suppose?"

Alice nodded. "I did. It had been empty for years again when I bought it last December. My dad managed most of the updates and I learned plenty along the way."

"I love it," Stella said. "This porch is perfect." She turned to her husband and asked David, "I don't remember a porch, do you?"

David shook his head. "And it's much more open than the last time we were here."

Alice loved hearing about the history of the Inn. She made a note to look further into their story. There would be information in the newspaper archives at the library.

"You mentioned your husband getting into astronomy?" David said, turning to a topic he was more versed on than Alice.

Alice nodded, suddenly missing Peter even more than usual. "He got me into astronomy too."

"Will we be meeting him?" David asked. "I'd love to talk to him about stars."

Sadness filled Alice's heart. It wasn't just her who would be missing his company this weekend. She knew that he would have enjoyed learning from David as well.

"No," she said, looking down into her teacup before meeting David's eye. "He passed away six months ago. Just before I purchased this Inn."

Stella gasped. "I'm so sorry to hear that."

Alice nodded. "Thank you," she whispered. There was never anything that anyone could say to make her admission of losing Peter any easier.

"This building seems to hold plenty of pain," Stella said. "Jack and Linda Lewis losing it to the fire, and rebuilding after the loss of your husband."

Alice didn't believe her ears. "Jack and Linda Lewis were the owners when you were to be married here?" she asked in disbelief.

Stella nodded. "I can't believe that after all these years I can still remember their names."

Alice couldn't move. Jack and Linda Lewis used to own the North Star Inn. Under a different name, but the same building for the same purpose.

"Honey, are you okay?" Stella asked, in her grandmotherly voice. "You look like you've seen a ghost."

CHAPTER FOURTEEN

That was not at all the conversation Brooke had prepared for as she'd sought out Stuart this morning. She'd been ready for a fight to win back her contract. And, if that didn't work, then for having to work with an adversary on what she considered her event.

Instead, Brooke was on cloud nine, wondering how long it would be until she heard from Donna to offer her the job back.

Brooke looked around and saw a taco truck parked down the street. She was starving, having hardly eaten any breakfast, the nerves of the morning making her forget that she was hungry. The scent of cooking taco meat made her stomach growl, and she crossed the street and placed an order.

As she waited for her lunch, sitting at a sticky picnic table in the shade, Brooke checked social media. What she saw sent her over the moon. Marci's statues were everywhere. Something about the coming together of the Inn and the sculptures was serendipitous, and Brooke had made that happen. The North Star Inn was trending locally on Twitter.

Brooke wanted to call Alice to tell her, knowing that she never touched Twitter. Facebook, yes. But Alice limited her social media to just one. And that, she barely updated.

When her name was called, Brooke grabbed her two tacos and practically inhaled them. They were mouth-wateringly delicious. She made a note to come back here any time she was in Burlington.

But now it was time to get back to work.

As Brooke walked back to her car, her phone rang. She knew who it would be before she even looked at it.

"Brooke Hastings," she answered.

"Brooke. It's Donna." Brooke smiled. That hadn't taken long. "Um... could you come back in? There's been a wrench thrown into everything."

"I'd be happy to." Brooke couldn't contain her joy and relief. She was going to get the contract after all. "Give me thirty-five minutes."

"Great. See you then." Donna hung up, her tone all business during the short phone call. Of course, she'd be disappointed that they'd have to spend more on the event. Was the country club hurting financially? Should Brooke be looking to expand her client base just in case, anyway?

She wouldn't worry about that right now. She got behind the wheel of her car as a wave of nausea passed over her. Maybe she should have taken her time eating those tacos. The moment passed and Brooke started the car for the drive back to Golden Bay.

Her exit was in sight on Highway 89 when Brooke's phone rang again. She didn't think it'd be Donna this time. She glanced at the screen, then answered on her Bluetooth.

"Hey honey," she said to Jared. She was way more

relaxed now than when they'd left the house this morning.

"I got it," he gushed. "I got the new contract. We just signed on for six books."

This news dwarfed Brooke's excitement over probably getting her own contract back. Jared had been looking to expand the number of authors he worked with for years, but the options had been limited. And he'd been picky. He wouldn't illustrate just any book. There had to be a bigger meaning to the story than just getting kids to read. And finding self-published children's book authors was difficult.

Like his last partnership—a series about a girl who pretended to be a superhero in her backyard with her dog. There were so few strong female characters in kids' books for little girls to aspire to. When Jared had found that author, he'd nearly bent over backward trying to win them over.

And it had worked. Brooke had read them to Emma daily until she'd outgrown them. They were some of her favorite books that Jared had done.

Now he was going after another strong little girl character who embodied past icons. Think Rosa Parks. Or Harriet Tubman. Or lesser-known women who had changed the course of history for the better, like Frances Perkins, the first woman to serve on the US Cabinet. They might not always have had a glorious career, but with some creative wording and catchy illustrations, picture books were a great introduction for kids to learn about everyday heroes and change makers.

"That's great! Congratulations!" Brooke wished she was with Jared as he shared the news. She knew he wouldn't have been able to wait. They had a tradition, though, that whenever either of them won a new client or signed a new contract, they would put on the same song and belt it out. It was their song. The song they first danced to at their wedding.

"Celebrate tonight?" Jared asked. "We can go out to dinner with the kids."

Brooke paused. That was the opposite of relaxing. Emma and Noah always ended up in some kind of argument, the entire restaurant usually relieved when they finally left.

"We could do that," she said hesitantly. "Or we could get takeout. Pizza?"

"Good idea. I always think going out is better than it ends up being. Are you headed home yet? We can celebrate without the kids first."

Brooke wished she was on her way home with the signed contract from Donna in her hand as another wave of nausea swept over her. This was too soon for the tacos to upset her stomach, right?

"I'm not on my way home yet. I just met with Stuart Randall, actually." As Brooke said his name, she realized Jared didn't know anything about what had been going on in her morning. She quickly caught him up, ending with Mitch not staying with his brother.

"Oh." He paused as he digested this bit of news. "Oh. That sounds worse for Celia."

"I know. I haven't told her yet." Brooke pulled off the highway and turned toward town.

"So, you're heading back to the country club now?" he confirmed.

"Yeah. Should be there in a few minutes." She turned left before asking, "Are you feeling okay today?"

"Fine. Why?" Concern filled his voice.

"My stomach feels off. I'm worried it's from last night. I would hate to have everyone who went to Alice's party get food poisoning. Nothing like that has ever happened with Otto before." Otto was her favorite caterer to work with, his food being the best, even while on the pricier side. It was worth the extra expense, in Brooke's opinion.

"You said you barely slept last night. Maybe you're just overtired," Jared said reassuringly.

Whenever Brooke's sleep was interrupted, she did get to the point where she wasn't even hungry, that was true. But this felt different. "Maybe," she told him, getting closer to the country club and needing to refocus on work.

"I hope you feel better. Call if you need anything."

"Will do. I'm almost to the club. I'll let you know what happens."

"Good luck." They didn't believe in jinxing each other.

"Thanks. Love you."

"Love you too," Jared said and hung up.

Brooke parked, took a deep breath to steady herself for whatever was going to come—the good or the bad, but she suspected things were turning in her favor. She took a second deep breath to push her nausea away that hadn't totally disappeared.

The fresh air did the job that deep breathing couldn't and Brooke's confidence returned. As soon as she entered the building, though, her nausea returned as well. She gave a quick wave to the receptionist and turned toward Donna's office. On the way, she stopped in the restroom.

Cold water on her face didn't help. Brooke leaned on the sink, feeling her stomach twist and turn. Was it the tacos she'd just eaten? Or Otto's food from last night?

Get it together, Brooke told herself while she looked in the mirror. Her small pep talk didn't help and she turned and raced into a stall where she lost her lunch.

Brooke took a minute to recompose herself, running

through the possibilities for feeling this sick. Otto. Tacos. Preschool germs. It could be anything. As she recovered and returned to the sink to wash her face again, Brooke made a mental note to ask Emma's teacher if there was a stomach bug going around. Just because summer was starting, didn't mean germs went on vacation. Germs in preschools still made their way around like wildfires.

Thankfully, Brooke found a mint in her pocketbook. She gave herself another minute for the color to return to her cheeks before she left to face Donna.

"Brooke," Donna said, standing. Her hesitations from this morning were no longer present. "Thanks for coming back."

"Of course." Brooke sat, anticipation building.

"There's been a change of plans and we'd like to offer you the Labor Day golf tournament as per your initial offer."

Brooke kept the smile off her face. She was going to fight for more.

"What happened?" she asked innocently.

Donna shook her head and leaned back in her chair. "I can't say. But the board wants you. They apologize for not picking you the first time."

Brooke's disappointment at losing the contract last night over email returned. Not only that, but the fear of not being able to cover her family's bills. With Jared landing today's deal that was less of an issue, but Donna didn't have to know that.

"How can I trust that this won't happen again?" Brooke asked. She wasn't walking away from this opportunity without trying to get a retainer.

A long sigh escaped from Donna. "What do you want, Brooke?"

Brooke smiled. "You know exactly what I want. I want to be held on retainer."

To Brooke's surprise, Donna returned her smile. "I told the board you'd ask for that."

Brooke waited but nothing more came. "And...?" she prompted.

"They're willing to offer you four events a year. The big ones. The ones you always do." Donna looked like that should be enough.

It wasn't.

Not this time.

Brooke pushed back. "And four smaller ones. I'm the best in Golden Bay, and apparently all the way down to Burlington, too. So keep me around. Let me do more."

Donna sighed again. "I told them you'd ask for more."

"You know me too well," Brooke teased, smiling.

"What kind of fees are you asking for? You'll still be a contractor."

Brooke nodded. Of course she wouldn't be an employee. She didn't want that. Brooke named a price and Donna didn't blink.

"Done."

Brooke was shocked. "You don't have to check with the board?"

"I asked them this morning what their breaking point was, and you came in just below it. I'll make sure to put the difference into a bonus."

This was moving faster than Brooke had expected. When Stuart turned down the contract for the Labor Day golf tournament, Donna must have scrambled to get enough board members on a conference call to get this all in place.

"All right then." Brooke offered her hand, the nerves in her belly subsiding now that they were in verbal agreement.

Donna shook her hand, then said, "I'll get the papers drawn up and get them to you next week. But you have my word—you are our person."

"Excellent. I'll see you next week then. Have a great weekend." Brooke knew she would now that her career was back on track.

"You too."

Brooke left Donna's office and finally let the joy show on her face. She gave a quick punch to the air, then looked around to make sure no one had seen it. The hallway was deserted, as it should be on a beautiful afternoon. Brooke wanted to be outside, too.

Before Brooke could bask in the glow of her success too much, she had to race back to the bathroom and into the same stall. Her stomach seemed to be trying to purge the last of her nerves and disappointment that were now past.

Brooke had to go home. All this getting sick was making her sweat and go weak. At the very least, she needed to brush her teeth and take a nap. After last night's sleeplessness and today's change in direction, she could finally relax again.

Then she needed a shower.

Brooke made it back to her car on wobbly legs. The nausea was gone but she had no energy. Thankfully, it was just a short drive home and there was never much traffic in Golden Bay.

As Brooke drove, she didn't think once about Donna or the Golden Bay Country Club. Instead, her mind filled with thoughts of her kids. Summer vacation was on the horizon and their family would be able to enjoy it more fully with the financial security Brooke and Jared had both secured today.

The only pharmacy in town came into view, and Brooke

pulled into the parking lot. She didn't need electrolytes or anti-nausea medicine.

She needed a pregnancy test.

The only times Brooke had ever been this sick and weak and tired were the three times she was pregnant. Emma had been the most challenging. She'd made up for it as an easy baby, but Brooke had also heard that each successive pregnancy for some women brought more morning sickness.

That had been the case for Brooke.

As she sat in the car, remembering those long weeks of eating hardly anything—to the point that she'd actually lost weight in the early part of Emma's pregnancy—Brooke thought about the possibility of being pregnant again. She opened the app on her phone that she used to track her periods and found that she was already two weeks late.

Life had kept moving forward and she hadn't even noticed.

For all the excitement today had brought, it didn't seem to be over yet.

In a fog, Brooke walked through the pharmacy until she found what she was looking for. The cashier didn't even make eye contact with her as she paid, too bored to notice what was going on around him.

Brooke had no memory of driving home, but she found herself parked in the garage, unable to take the next step.

"Are you okay?" Jared asked, coming into the garage. Brooke opened her door and forced herself to get out of the car. "I heard the garage but you never came inside."

Brooke wasn't sure how long she'd sat in the car before Jared came out. It could have been one minute or fifteen. She was not ready to tell him what was really eating her. Not until she knew exactly what was going on, though she was pretty sure by now.

"My stomach is still off. You're feeling okay?"

Jared looked at her with concern in her eyes. "I'm fine. Can I bring anything in for you?"

Brooke grabbed her pocketbook and headed inside. "I don't think I have anything else. I'm going to go lie down for a bit."

"Let me know if you need anything," Jared told her as he followed her into the house, closing the door behind them both. "And we can skip pizza tonight if you want. Maybe something lighter."

Brooke couldn't think about eating. Not only because her stomach was getting revenge on her, but because adding a fourth baby to their family was not part of their plan.

She'd already made a mental list of all the things they'd need—replacing most of the baby gear they'd already given away because they were done having kids. A bigger car was the biggest of her worries, but everything else added up, too. A crib. Years of diapers. Car seats as the baby grew.

Childcare.

Emma was a year away from kindergarten, a light at the end of the tunnel, and they'd have to start over.

In the master bathroom, Brooke took the pregnancy test out of her pocketbook and sat on the toilet. She had just a few minutes left of trying to fool herself into believing her body was hers alone. She already knew there was another baby growing in her womb. But she needed definitive proof to fully believe it.

She peed on the stick and placed the cap back on, then lay it on a tissue on the edge of the tub while she brushed her teeth. Brooke took her time until she was sure the test would be finished.

She turned to the tub, her future staring back at her.

CHAPTER FIFTEEN

Stella and David took their leave from the porch just as Astrid and Karl came up from the rooms below. "We'll leave you with your other guests. Thanks for the cord," David said as the older couple returned downstairs.

Alice was in no mental or emotional position to spend more time focused on her guests. Learning the history of both the Inn and Jack and Linda Lewis had thrown her for a loop.

Thankfully, Astrid and Karl felt the same about sitting with a stranger. They turned down Alice's offer of fresh tea and blueberry bread, probably antsy to get back to the privacy of their room on the first day of their honeymoon.

Alice ran their credit card and brought them their own welcome folder before they asked about the beach.

"Is it available to us?" Karl asked, pointing toward the peninsula south of the Inn.

"Of course." There was a sloping grassy lawn leading down to a private beach, chairs and tables setup for her guests. "You're welcome to swim. And I can point you toward canoeing and kayaking if you're interested. And sailing. I can get that all set up with the Golden Bay Country Club."

Brooke working the events for the country club had helped Alice secure access to their equipment.

"Maybe tomorrow," Astrid said, her eyes never leaving her new husband's face.

The young newlyweds practically ran out of the porch and downstairs before Alice heard them leaving from the lower exit to find some peace and quiet on the shores of Lake Champlain.

Alice didn't leave her chair on the porch. She was stunned with Stella's news of Jack and Linda Lewis owning this very building fifty years ago.

Footsteps on the stairs brought Alice back to the present. Stella and David returned from downstairs and peeked their heads out to the porch. "We're going to walk into town. Don't wait up for us. We might stay there through dinner."

Alice waved. "You have a key. Let yourself in whenever you return. All the lights are on timers and motion sensors so you'll never be left in the dark."

"Thank you for everything," Stella said before they turned and headed toward the front of the Inn.

Alice was alone. Peace and quiet enveloped her, letting her thoughts charge in any direction without her choosing.

For the last six months, Alice had been living a race. The opening of the North Star Inn had been her sole focus. That uninterrupted attention had served two purposes—to get her business up and running, but also to take her mind off of Peter's passing.

Now, Alice sat alone with no guests to care for, a fridge full of food for the weekend's breakfasts, and nothing she urgently had to do. Thoughts of her past overwhelmed her, unbidden and unwelcome.

What would Peter say about Jack and Linda Lewis's gift?

What would Peter think about them owning the Inn half a century ago?

Alice couldn't push the questions from her mind. Questions she would never have answers to. She would have to navigate these uncharted waters on her own. She would have to build her own lifeboat using the love Peter had left behind.

Standing, Alice took a deep breath and cleaned up the last of the mugs and plates. The afternoon stretched before her and she wasn't going to sit here wallowing in what she didn't have.

Once the dishes were loaded in the dishwasher, Alice took the letter from her birth parents out of the folder from Mr. Thompson.

She held it for a long moment before reading it again, trying her best to live up to her birth parents' request—keep an open heart. Alice had closed her heart to them decades ago when she hadn't been able to track them down. Now she could feel it opening just the slightest bit, a crack where there had been none.

By the end of the letter, Alice's eyes were filled with tears and her heart filled with wonder. Wonder at who Jack and Linda truly were. Wonder at the coincidence of growing up in the town of her birth. Wonder at their lives all intersecting at the North Star Inn.

Alice put the letter back carefully—she did not want to lose it—and headed to the front door. She finally had the start of information about her birth parents and she intended to learn more.

Alice drove to the Golden Bay Library to start her search for answers about Linda and Jack. Stella's information about the fire at the Inn fifty years ago was the place to begin.

"Hi Alice," Irene, the library director, greeted her from the front desk.

"Hi Irene," Alice returned. She'd seen her friend last night at the launch party but felt she'd lived a whole lifetime since then.

"Congratulations again on such a success last night. I think everyone who's come in today has commented on the sculptures."

Alice smiled. "It was a good night, wasn't it?"

Irene nodded. "Marci has such talent. Did you know that sculpture upstairs is one of her early works?"

Alice shook her head. "She's come a long way." Alice looked up above the upstairs railing at the sculpture she'd seen dozens of times. It paled in comparison to the huge sculptures now sitting on the west lawn of the Inn.

"She certainly has," Irene agreed. "Will hasn't stopped talking about it. He has called twice already today." Irene shook her head.

Alice scrunched her eyebrows together. She'd seen him this morning at the farmer's market. How could he have that much to say about last night? "I'm glad he enjoyed himself."

"I think he'd enjoy himself no matter where he was as long as you were there." Irene gave Alice a pointed look.

"I don't think so," Alice rebutted. "We're too old to be caught up in someone else like that."

Irene laughed. "I don't think so, Alice. Will has liked you since he was fifteen. I don't think anything's changed."

Alice didn't believe her friend.

"I told him to give you some space. Peter's only been

gone six months. That feels like no time when you've lost the one you loved." Irene's eyes got a faraway look and Alice knew she was remembering her own deceased husband.

But Irene was right. Alice still forgot sometimes that Peter would never come home again.

Getting back to business, Irene asked, "Is there anything I can help you find?"

"Actually, yes. I'm looking for any newspaper articles from fifty years ago in Golden Bay. I just learned about a fire at the Inn then and want to learn more about it," Alice explained.

Irene stood from behind her computer and met Alice on the other side of the desk. "Sure. We have subscriptions to some of the bigger newspaper archives—"

"Just local," Alice interrupted.

Irene nodded. "Okay. We'll have to get on the computer. It's so rare that someone comes in looking for old papers from Golden Bay. Let's see if I can find them."

Alice followed Irene to a computer and watched as she searched for what she considered nearly ancient history. Not that she thought of herself as that old—the fire she was looking for occurred just before she was born; her parents might even remember the event—but in the ever-changing world of news stories, fifty years ago may as well be the Ice Age.

"Here. What year did you say? Fifty years ago?" Irene confirmed. Alice nodded. "Do you have a month?"

"Before June. April or May, I think." Alice knew that Stella and David were married in June, so the fire must have happened before then.

"Okay." Irene tapped on the keyboard some more and then stood. "Here are March, April, and May for you to look through. If you need more help, you know where to find me."

Alice took the vacated seat and said, "Thank you." She was heading down this path without looking back.

The newspapers were arranged chronologically from March first, so Alice scanned headlines starting there. Nothing caught her attention until mid-April, where she saw a building that could be the Inn. It was nearly unrecognizable with all the smoke, fire, and water damage.

Alice didn't know how to print the article, so she leaned toward the computer to read it on the screen. When she finished, she found three more from that week giving more information about the origin of the fire.

Stella had heard that arson had been the cause of the fire, and she wasn't wrong. From what Alice could piece together from the articles, the owners—who she confirmed were indeed Jack and Linda Lewis—had returned home to a fire on the lower level of the Inn. They had done everything they could to stop the spread, but an accelerant seemed to be in play. By the time the fire department arrived, the fire had spread upstairs.

The building had been salvageable, but just barely. It would need to be gutted before it was habitable again. And with arson being the cause, the Lewises were not entitled to insurance money.

Alice leaned back in her chair. Linda would have been three months pregnant. For the next six months, until Alice's birth in October, Linda and Jack must have struggled with what to do.

Stella's conversation rang in Alice's ears. *They lost everything... I kept putting myself in their shoes.*

What would Alice have done if she and Peter were suddenly homeless and jobless while pregnant with Viv?

Alice shook her head, trying to take that thought back. That wasn't how her life had turned out, and she was thankful.

But she could suddenly see that her start to life had not been as simple as her own kids' beginnings.

Alice remembered the letter from Jack and Linda, too. *Things that were out of our control made it clear that we would be unable to give you the life you deserved.*

The fire at the Inn had changed the course of their lives. They'd gone from excitement over starting a family that they'd desperately wanted for years, to making the horrifying decision to give their child up for adoption in the hopes of a better life.

Alice could now see that that decision was the final act of love Jack and Linda gave her.

On wobbly legs, Alice left the computer in a daze. She passed the desk, thankful it was empty so she wouldn't have to make small talk with Irene—one of her best friends and someone she'd known practically all her life—and headed back to her car. She sat in the quiet before driving home, all the pieces of her life suddenly falling into place this afternoon.

Her birth parents hadn't abandoned her, like she'd felt as a teen. They had given her the gift of a family that could provide for her.

They hadn't turned their backs on her. They'd given her the freedom to be her true self without feeling a responsibility to the people who had given her life.

Still, they could have reached out sooner. Maybe it was selfish, like Linda suggested in her letter, that they hadn't ever met Alice. But as a mother, Alice could better understand their decisions. To make the excruciating decision to give your daughter away once was enough. To do it again later in life would be too much.

Back at the Inn, Alice cleaned up the folder from Mr. Thompson. He would be in touch, he'd said, and she would deal with everything then. The house in southern Vermont wasn't going anywhere until she gave him the go-ahead. She slid the folder into a drawer in her office and told herself to forget about it.

Alice saw that Astrid and Karl were still down at the beach, and there was no sign of Stella and David. She had the rest of the afternoon and evening to do whatever she needed.

Peter's ashes had been spread in various places around Golden Bay, and she wanted nothing more than to talk to him. Alice walked toward the shore past the sculpture garden, needing to tell him about Jack and Linda Lewis.

CHAPTER SIXTEEN

Celia saw Cori outside the front door and she went to unlock it. It was time to open Celia's Bookshelf back up to customers after suddenly closing so she could begin to reconcile with her husband.

"Everything okay?" Cori asked, her eyebrows scrunched together in confusion. Celia never closed the bookstore in the middle of the day.

"Fine," Celia said, false cheer dripping from her words.

"Hi Mitch." The teen employee had no idea what was going on between Celia and Mitch, and Celia intended to keep it that way.

"I have to run out with Mitch for a bit. I'm so sorry to leave you alone here again. Thank you for closing yesterday."

"No problem," Cori reassured Celia before Celia could expel the rest of her verbal vomit. As long as she was talking, Celia didn't have to face the reality of Mitch's words.

I haven't been staying with Stuart.

"I should be back in an hour," Celia said, though she really had no idea how long she'd be away.

"Don't worry. I've got this." Cori smiled and dropped her things behind the desk. "Take your time."

Celia released the breath she'd been holding and grabbed her bag. "I don't have my car," she told her husband. "Can I ride with you?"

Celia would have loved nothing better to drive separately to collect her thoughts before she found out what was truly going on with Mitch. Somehow, she could accept that he had a twelve-year-old son he'd just found out about easier than the fact that he wasn't staying with his brother.

"Of course." Mitch pulled Celia close, his arm around her waist, and Celia stiffened. "It's not what you think," he whispered into her hair.

Celia wanted to believe him. She wanted to relax in his embrace. She wanted to return to the place they had been four months ago before any of this had ripped apart her marriage and her life.

Mitch let go of Celia as they walked out of the bookstore and toward his truck. Celia took one look at his work truck and asked, "Will you have room for everything with all your equipment in the back?"

Mitch opened the driver's door and climbed in. When Celia was in the passenger seat, he answered, "I hardly have anything. It'll all fit."

There was one question banging around Celia's mind, trying to break its way out. But she wasn't ready for more truth bombs. Not yet.

"Are you going to ask why I haven't been staying with Stuart?" Mitch asked.

Golden Bay passed by the window at a speed Celia rarely experienced in the summer. Her world was small, mostly sticking to the bookstore, home, and her sisters' homes. Everything was within easy cycling distance. Moving at this speed nearly made her sick.

Or maybe that was just the anticipation of whatever was coming next.

"Why haven't you been staying with Stuart?" Celia asked in one breath. All Celia could think was that he'd been staying with Lisa and Dylan. Or at least close to them. She was going to have to learn to trust him again, and that was going to take some time.

"Stuart and Crystal told me that I had a perfectly good place to live and that I could pack up and tell you the truth. They said that I should be living with you, not with them."

Celia was stunned. While she'd never been close to Stuart and hardly knew his wife, Crystal, they had been on her side all along. A part of her had been afraid to go to Stuart's to look for Mitch because she didn't want to cross Stuart.

She had been so wrong.

Anger bloomed in her chest. Anger at Mitch for staying away, and anger at Stuart for not coming to her directly. She clenched and unclenched her fists before asking, "So where have you been staying?"

By this time, they were nearing Burlington and Mitch turned onto a side street. Instead of answering, he made a couple more turns and pulled to the side of the road next to a large house.

"Here," he said, looking toward the old Victorian that could house at least a dozen individuals.

Celia shook her head. "What is this place?"

"I'll show you."

The love was back in Mitch's eyes, and Celia told herself to trust him. It wouldn't be easy, but she was committed to saving their marriage. Mitch had knocked out one of the stabilizing pillars, but it was up to both of them to rebuild it.

Celia exited the truck and Mitch met her on the sidewalk, taking her hand and leading her to the front door. He let himself inside and Celia was once again thrown for a loop.

The house smelled like her grandmother's house—musty mothballs. She didn't dislike the smell, but it was certainly distinct and brought back memories of playing dress-up with Brooke as a child.

Mitch pulled her out of her memories and led her upstairs. "This is it," he said. There was a single suitcase lying on the bed, packed. "I packed this morning just in case you'd have me back."

Celia remembered the morning back in February when he'd packed that suitcase. She had biked to work that morning despite the numbing cold. It had taken hours for her fingers to feel normal again. And she'd chickened out and called Brooke for a ride home after work. Biking in the dark of winter was too painful, even if it numbed the pain of Mitch leaving her.

"But whose house is this?" Celia asked, still confused about what was going on.

"Luella's," Mitch said, like Celia would know who that was. "I'll introduce you."

Mitch brought the suitcase downstairs and Celia followed hesitantly. This afternoon had already rocked her world. She wasn't ready for another surprise.

He left the suitcase by the front door and then headed into the rear of the house. Celia peaked through doorways as they passed. The house was immaculate. And huge.

"I thought I heard your footsteps." The woman's voice

reached Celia's ears before she saw her. But when she did, any concerns about Mitch's possible infidelity left her.

Mitch approached Luella and kissed her cheek. Celia didn't do the same. Not because the woman looked to be in her nineties and was bound to a wheelchair, but because she'd never seen her before and kissing wasn't Celia's go-to greeting.

"You must be Celia," Luella said, a smile lighting up her face. "I had hoped I'd get to meet you this afternoon."

Celia looked to Mitch with more and more questions burning in her mind. This elderly woman knew about her? How much had he revealed about their marriage?

"Mitch told me last night that he was going to see the woman he loved today. He wasn't sure what you'd say. I guess you told him you also love him. That's good." Luella smiled. "We only get one life, and there's no time to hold on to grudges. Forgiveness is freeing."

The smile on Luella's face softened Celia toward the woman. She smiled back. "I did tell him I love him," she said, no longer worried about what she knew. Luella was right—there was only time for love. Mitch may have made a mistake, but Celia had loved him all along.

"I'm moving back home," Mitch told her. "But don't hesitate to call if you need anything else fixed. I'm happy to come by to help."

"Don't be silly. You have your own life to live. I'll just have to convince my great-grandson to take a break from those silly video games he thinks are so important."

Mitch leaned down and kissed Luella on the cheek again. "Thank you for taking me in."

"It's been a pleasure, young man."

Celia watched the whole exchange in awe. She'd always known Mitch had a loving side, but she thought he reserved it for herself alone. She was seeing her husband through new eyes.

"Don't let that man get away," Luella said to Celia with a wave.

"I don't plan to," Celia promised her.

Then Mitch took her hand as if they were leaving the wedding chapel and waltzed down the hall and out the front door, not even breaking stride when he picked up his suitcase.

Celia was struck numb. Mitch climbed into the driver's seat again after he tossed his suitcase into the bed of the truck.

"What was all that?" Celia asked, still trying to put everything together.

How had Mitch ended up living at Luella's?

Why did he offer to come back to help?

"I kind of fell into meeting her. I was working next door when a teenager had trouble starting a lawn mower. I offered to help him, and he kind of unloaded on me about his great-grandmother. He did the yardwork but she always asked him to do other stuff around the house and he had no idea how to help. I kind of offered to help in exchange for a room once it became clear that she lived alone but probably shouldn't." Mitch drove as he spoke, never taking his eyes off the road as they made their way back to Golden Bay.

"Is she going to be okay without you?" Celia asked, suddenly finding herself concerned for Luella's well-being.

Mitch shrugged. "I'll check in on her in a few days to make sure she has the help she needs. Her family is all local, but they have a lot going on. And she has an aide who comes every morning and evening. But, otherwise, she's alone for much of the day. It doesn't seem like the way for someone her age to live."

Celia agreed. "I'm glad you found her. It sounds like you both needed each other while you were there."

Mitch turned and met Celia's eye. They shared a smile and Celia knew they'd be okay.

The rest of the ride back to the condo was quiet as Celia thought about their future. The biggest question was how to incorporate Dylan into their lives. How was Lisa going to feel about Celia being around? Would she be a step-mother?

That wasn't at all how Celia had pictured motherhood, but maybe it would be for the best. Babies scared her. This way she could skip that stage.

These decisions weren't up to her alone, though. She and Mitch were a team. They would work this out together. With Lisa and Dylan, of course.

Mitch parked in the small lot in front of the condos and turned off the engine. "Are you okay?" he asked and took her hand in his.

Celia nodded. "Just thinking about Dylan." Mitch remained silent so Celia continued. "I can accept that you don't want a baby. I totally get that. But I'll love Dylan because he's your son and I love you."

Mitch whispered, "Thank you," and kissed her.

Celia felt her world begin to right itself. The last four months had turned everything upside down, but with Mitch back and the two of them working together, things were starting to fall back into place.

They left the truck and Celia walked up the front steps to unlock their home as Mitch grabbed his suitcase. He met her on the porch and Celia paused. This felt like a huge moment for them. She was welcoming him back into their home after a big mistake.

Her lungs filled with air and she unlocked the door,

opening their home and her heart to whatever the future held.

Just before they walked inside together, a car pulled into the lot and parked. "New neighbors?" Mitch asked.

When he'd left, the middle condo had been vacant and on the market.

"Just last night, actually," Celia told him.

Mitch stared as a man exited the driver's side. Celia saw recognition cross Mitch's face, and she knew she was right—she did know him from somewhere. But she still didn't know from where.

"You know who that is?" Mitch asked, excitement in his voice.

Celia shook her head. "Can't place his face."

"Seth. We played college basketball together." Mitch was laughing as he told her. He raised his hand and waved to their new neighbor.

Recognition registered on Seth's face and he called up to Mitch, "Hey man. You live here?"

"I do." The two men briefly caught up after Celia was introduced and she went inside. She would let Mitch tell her about Seth after. She wanted to make sure their home was somewhat put together for his return.

A few minutes later, Mitch joined her inside, shock written across his whole body.

"What happened?" Celia asked.

"I totally lost touch with Seth after college, even though we'd been really close," he started. Mitch sat down on the couch and Celia joined him, not wanting to be apart any longer.

"He married his college girlfriend," he continued. "But she passed away when their daughter was three. Now he's raising her alone. She's twelve, just like Dylan."

Celia was surprised at the coincidence. She had to admit that would be much harder than what she and Mitch were facing. They had each other. And Dylan. Seth had only his daughter.

"I'm glad he's next door," Mitch said. "And I'm glad I'm home."

Celia leaned into Mitch and he wrapped his arm around her. She felt like she was finally home again, too.

She couldn't stay there all afternoon, though. She still had a bookstore to run. "I have to get back to work," she told him, but didn't make a move to get up.

"Me too," he said. "Have to make a dent in everything before the days get too hot."

Mowing lawns was much more enjoyable in the cool air of early June than the heat of late July, but it always had to be done.

"Before we leave," Celia started, "I have to tell you that my parents are on their way home. They want everyone at Alice's Inn tomorrow for dinner. I was hoping... you'd... come?"

Celia wasn't sure how he'd feel about seeing her whole family so soon after returning home. She would certainly be hesitant to jump right back into Mitch's family events if she'd been the one to walk out all those months ago.

Mitch nodded. "Can I sit this one out?"

Celia sat up and looked at her husband. "I would really like you to be there. We can take that first step forward together."

Mitch remained silent. "Let me drive you back to work," he said when he finally stood.

This wasn't the answer Celia was hoping for. If he was going to make everything right, then they had to face her family sooner rather than later.

They rode to the bookstore in silence, Celia holding out hope that Mitch would make up his mind by the time they arrived. And that he'd make the right decision.

He pulled to the side of the road across from Celia's Bookshelf and turned off the truck.

"You'll come tomorrow, right?" she asked.

Mitch sighed. "I'm not sure I'm ready to face your sisters and parents."

Celia wasn't going to let him off the hook that easily. "If not tomorrow, then when?"

Mitch shook his head. "I don't know. Can I think about it?"

In Celia's opinion, there was nothing to think about. Mitch was either coming home and they were a team, facing everything head-on together, or he wasn't fully back.

"I'd really like you to be there," she told him.

Mitch didn't answer right away. "I'll think about it," he said again.

Celia realized this was the best she was going to get right now. Instead of arguing after just barely making amends, she nodded and headed across the street to work.

CHAPTER SEVENTEEN

Brooke walked out of the bathroom and into the bedroom. It was empty. Jared was probably getting some work done in his office before he had to pick up the kids from school. They were constantly racing against the clock of childcare.

A tug-of-war played out in Brooke's mind as she sat on the end of their bed. To tell Jared now or later? One truth stuck out, though—she had to tell him.

Brooke considered breaking the news to him while he was on Cloud Nine, lightening the blow slightly. Or she could let the family celebrate his contract—as well as Brooke's with the country club—before the hammer fell. Then Jared walked into the room.

"What's that?" he asked, pointing to Brooke's hand holding the pregnancy test and sealing their fate as a family of six.

Silently, Brooke handed the proof to her husband and watched the reality of this twist of fate sink in.

"You're... pregnant?" Jared asked, as incredulously sounding as Brooke felt.

Brooke's head nodded all on its own without her needing to tell it to move. She was numb.

"How?" he asked.

Giggles erupted from Brooke, as if she was a middle schooler talking about kissing her first boyfriend. "I think you know how that happens," she sputtered in a fit of laughter.

Jared didn't seem to find this as hysterical as Brooke did. He turned to face her. "I thought we agreed to stop at three kids?"

"Oh, we agreed. This was not planned. I've been taking the pill." Brooke thought back over the past month. There had been at least two days in there where she'd totally forgotten to take her daily pill. She'd tried to avoid anything intimate once she realized she was behind, but she could have gotten sloppy. Or missed a third day. It was hard to keep up with everything.

And whenever the kids were all in bed early, Brooke and Jared took advantage of the quiet house to fully enjoy each other. It wasn't like they had ample opportunity now that Tina stayed up later.

"I guess I should have taken care of things from my end," Jared admitted, and Brooke's heart bloomed with love for him.

So many men pinned the fault of unwanted pregnancies on the woman, but Jared took half of the blame. It took two to tango, after all.

"I guess we both could have done more to prevent this," Brooke agreed, taking Jared's hand. "But here we are."

"What are we going to do?" he asked, concern coming through thick in those six words.

Brooke had been given a head start on thinking about this. Maybe only a few hours more than Jared had, but her thoughts had headed down this very road earlier this afternoon.

"We'll need a bigger car," she said.

Jared groaned.

"And another four years of childcare."

He groaned again. "Just when Emma was almost done."

"I know." Brooke squeezed his hand. "We can do this."

Brooke wasn't sure *how* they would do this, but she knew they would. There was no other option.

Jared slowly nodded. "You're right. We can. Maybe your parents can help?"

Brooke didn't mean to start laughing again, but she did. "Maybe. I think I'll be due in February sometime, so they probably won't be around then. They'll be in Florida."

"Maybe they'll skip next winter in Florida. It's another grandkid, and they can't seem to get enough."

It was a possibility they could explore, but Brooke knew they shouldn't count on it.

"We just need a few months of help before we send it to Growing Daisies," Jared said, trying to rationalize how simple it sounded taking care of a newborn. They both knew it wasn't always easy.

"We'll cross that road later. No one even knows about it yet."

Jared turned and took hold of Brooke's other hand, the positive pregnancy test now clasped in both of their hands. "You could take time off, you know," he said, his eyes almost pleading with her to say yes.

Brooke sighed. "You know as well as I do that I can't. I almost just lost the country club's contract. Now I'll be on retainer. If I don't follow through, I'll disappear. Other event planners will swoop right in to snatch up anything I turn down."

"I can make up the difference. Today's deal will help. And I can be less picky. I can draw for anyone, we both know that. I just don't like to. I can put my name out there more. I know how tired you are with all the nighttime nursing. It's not fair to ask you to do that and work full-time."

He was right; it wasn't fair. But it was reality. Brooke had never taken much time off after having a baby. She was lucky, though. She could usually work from home with a small baby. They slept so much at that age that she could still be productive. She'd had to wear Tina and Noah while they napped, but Emma had been easy and would sleep anywhere. If they were lucky, this baby would be easy, too.

"We'll figure it out. Let's take it one day at a time for now," Brooke said, knowing she wouldn't take much time off. "And first things first, we have to get the baby on childcare lists. Growing Daisies, for sure. But maybe we should check out some others, just in case. Maybe there's one that's less expensive."

Jared released Brooke's hands. "We've done that. Growing Daisies has been good to us. We should stick with them."

Brooke didn't want to argue about the details. She had to let it all go and take a nap. "Do you still like the name Liam for a boy?" she asked. That had been their pick for Emma, who had surprised them with her gender. Emma hadn't cooperated for the ultrasound so they hadn't managed to learn ahead of time if they were having a girl or boy. But based on how sick Brooke felt, she was sure they were having another boy. Noah had given her a run for her money.

Jared nodded. "And Carley for a girl?"

Brooke grimaced. "Really?"

"What? You don't like that?" They were both smiling

and more relaxed suddenly, talking about the seemingly smaller things that came with having a baby.

"We have time. But, no. Not Carley." Brooke laughed.

"I just had an idea," Jared said, changing the subject. "What if we asked Alice for help with early childcare? We know she's great with babies. And she'll be home at the Inn."

Brooke fell back onto the bed, ready to close her eyes and take a nap. She was exhausted for so many reasons—last night's sleeplessness, today's excitement, and the body-ravaging tired that came with early pregnancy.

"Being home isn't the same as being available," Brooke said with her eyes closed. "This is her opening weekend of a huge new venture. We can't put more on her plate."

"We don't have to ask her right now. But maybe once things are more up and running?" He didn't sound as hopeful anymore.

It was true that Alice was great with babies and that she loved them. Her two daughters had grown into wonderful young women, thanks in large part to Alice's patient parenting. Brooke often wished she had more patience.

But asking Alice to be a babysitter while she worked from home made no more sense to Brooke than Brooke working from home with her baby with her.

"We'll figure it out," she said again. After a sigh that emptied her lungs, Brooke asked, "I checked with you about dinner at the Inn tomorrow, right?" The day had been so crazy that she couldn't remember who knew what.

"No." Brooke felt Jared flop onto the bed next to her. She turned her head and opened her eyes.

"My parents are getting back tomorrow and want dinner with everyone. Celia told me this morning. Do you have anything?" Brooke almost hoped that he'd made plans she didn't know about so they'd have an excuse not to go. Not because she didn't want to see her parents—she knew the kids would be overjoyed to see their grandparents again —but because she was just too tired.

"Nothing. What can we bring?" Jared asked.

"No idea. Hopefully just ourselves." Brooke closed her eyes again.

"You need to rest," Jared said, stating the obvious.

With her eyes still closed, Brooke felt Jared stand. "What are we going to tell the kids?" she asked before he left the room.

"About what? Dinner?"

"No. About the baby." Without meaning to, Brooke placed her hands over her abdomen. She couldn't feel life growing inside of her yet—unless she considered her nausea and exhaustion—but she knew it was there.

"Nothing yet." Jared was so matter-of-fact with his answer that Brooke sat up.

"Nothing? I meant, do we tell them all together or one at a time since they all have such different understandings of how babies are made?"

"When did you want to tell them?" Jared asked. "Tonight?"

Brooke nodded. "They'll notice that I feel different and they should know why."

Jared didn't say anything for a moment and the silence made Brooke uneasy. They hardly ever disagreed on big parenting decisions. "What if we lose the baby? Shouldn't we wait a while?"

"I've never had any trouble before," Brooke said, though she knew that didn't mean she wouldn't now. She was on the older side for becoming pregnant so her risks were higher. "I want them to know what's going on."

"Why don't you get some rest? The kids will be home soon and it won't be so quiet. I'll get some work done. Maybe I'll take them to the playground when I pick them up so you get some extra time alone."

Brooke lay back again. She didn't even have the energy to crawl up to the pillows. "Thanks," she said, still thinking about when and what to tell the kids about having a new sibling.

The door closed as Jared left the room and Brooke drifted off to sleep.

CHAPTER EIGHTEEN

Alice woke early and fully rested. She'd spent hours at the shores of Lake Champlain just past the sculpture garden where she'd once spread some of Peter's ashes. The magnitude of the day had caught up with her there—the official opening of the North Star Inn and receiving not only the news of who her birth parents were, but that they had passed away and left her everything they owned.

The opening of the Inn was almost bittersweet as she'd sat with her eyes closed, waiting to feel Peter's presence that never came. Their dream had come to fruition, a dream they knew Peter would never see. His support and ideas were integral to Alice even taking the first step in purchasing the building, and she could see him everywhere in the changes she'd made—the tables in the dining room made from a tree on the property they'd shared for decades; the names of the rooms representing their favorite constellations; the kitchen that was nearly identical to the kitchen they'd cooked meals in for their growing family.

Now Alice was alone.

She might have her doubts sometimes, but she knew she could do this.

Saturday morning dawned bright. Alice rose to eat before her guests were up and enjoyed a cup of coffee on the screened porch in the silence she loved so much. Mornings when her kids were young had been difficult, everyone needing something as soon as she was out of bed. Now she'd give anything to have that chaos back—to have Peter, Viv, and Nora all under the same roof with her.

The coffee went down easily and Alice returned to the kitchen for a thick slice of Heather's bread, toasted to perfection, with butter and jam and a side of sliced strawberries. She didn't want to overdo breakfast when she had a full morning ahead of her.

Breakfast at the Inn started at eight, but guests were welcome to come down and help themselves to a fruit bowl and coffee any time. Alice was barely finished with her toast in the kitchen when she heard footsteps next door in the dining room. She suspected it wouldn't be Astrid and Karl, who seemed to be basking in each other's company in their newlywed state.

Alice peeked into the dining room and was not surprised to see Stella and David sitting down with coffee next to the window. She finished cleaning up her own dishes before joining them in the dining room to find out what she could make them for breakfast.

"Good morning," she said, surprising them both, based on their expressions.

"You walk on silent feet," Stella said, a welcoming smile nearly inviting Alice to pull up a chair like an old friend.

"You slept well?" Alice asked. These were the very first guests to come to the dining room for breakfast, and she wanted everything to be just perfect.

"Like a baby," Stella said. "Though I've never really understood that expression. In my experience, plenty of babies don't sleep well."

Alice chuckled in agreement, unsure if Stella had slept well or not now.

"I slept wonderfully," Stella clarified. "Woke with the sun, just like at home."

"Glad to hear it. Can I get you anything for breakfast? I can also bring a French press of coffee if you prefer. Or help yourself to the coffee maker whenever you want."

"A French press would be great. Dark roast, please," David said.

"Sure. And breakfast is eggs any way you want, toast from local bread, local strawberries—the first of the season—and juice. I'll get the coffee going and you can think about what you'd like."

Alice left before either of them could keep her longer. She didn't want to be talking about breakfast with Stella; she wanted to ask her if she remembered anything else about Jack and Linda Lewis from fifty years ago.

Moments later, Alice returned with the coffee and placed it on the table between the elderly couple.

"Are you all right?" Stella asked as Alice backed up to give them space. "You seem different this morning. Not as relaxed."

Alice was surprised that Stella picked up that closely on her mood. She wasn't as relaxed, but only because she wanted to ask Stella about the Lewises but didn't want to take over their anniversary weekend.

"I understand this is your opening weekend; is everything going smoothly?" Stella asked, seeming to fish for the cause of Alice's change in mood.

Alice smiled. "Everything is going swimmingly," she

assured her guests. It was very thoughtful of Stella to check in on the running of the Inn, but Alice didn't want that to be their focus. She would wait until later to ask about Jack and Linda. At least until after breakfast. "Have you decided what you'd like for breakfast?"

David spoke up first. "Two poached eggs with everything else you mentioned."

Stella hesitated, looking like she wanted to ask Alice more questions, but instead said, "Two over easy, please."

Alice nodded. "I'll get them going right now. Enjoy the view and your coffee."

Alice took a dozen eggs from the fridge and couldn't resist making herself some while she cooked for her guests. Within minutes, the water was hot for poaching eggs and the toast had popped up. She flipped Stella's eggs—only breaking one yolk, then keeping that one for herself—and added sliced berries to each plate.

It all looked delicious. Alice smiled as she put the hot eggs on each plate and carried them to the table against the window. "Be careful; the eggs are hot," she warned.

Stella and David thanked her and picked up their forks. Alice retreated back to the kitchen where she toasted another slice of bread and put her own egg on top. When she finished, she snuck around through the sitting room to the screened porch to read the local newspaper that came every weekend. There, she could keep one eye on the dining room in case Stella or David needed anything, and she'd hear if Astrid and Karl came up from their bedroom. She didn't expect them for hours still.

Alice unfolded the four-page paper and read the top article. To her surprise, the newly unveiled sculpture garden was front and center—above the fold. She'd never spoken to a reporter, but it seemed Marci had. Alice was excited for her friend, and for the publicity.

There was no charge for the public to visit the sculpture garden. She wanted it to be a welcoming place for both guests and locals alike. Alice didn't expect many Golden Bay residents to stay at the North Star Inn, but she wanted them to feel welcome and included in her business. She'd spent her whole life in Golden Bay and there was hardly a resident she didn't know. It was a small community; opening her west lawn to everyone felt like the least she could do.

Alice read the article, noticing that her name came up several times. She was surprised she hadn't been contacted for a statement. She made a note to check her messages, something she would have to get better about doing so she didn't miss any possible reservations.

As Alice finished the article, she noticed Stella and David fill their coffee cups and stand. They left their dishes —Alice was glad they didn't try to clean them up themselves—and came out to the screened porch.

"Can I get you anything else?" Alice asked, getting up and refolding her paper.

"No. It was all delicious," Stella said, sitting on the small couch, David joining her.

"Those are your statues," David pointed out, picking up the newspaper.

"Yes. I guess Marci—the artist—gave an interview. I never even noticed a photographer or reporter out there." Alice looked at the photos again and realized they were probably taken yesterday when she was out at the library.

"I love them," Stella said, turning to look at them. "Is the artist local?"

Alice told them about Marci, her friend from childhood. Marci had left for several years but had returned after a messy divorce more than twenty years ago. They'd reconnected then, Alice offering as much support as she could in a life challenge she hadn't experienced. It was hard to relate to marrying someone you could fall out of love with when she was so in love with Peter. But she'd stuck by her friend's side and they'd grown closer over the years. Marci had become like an aunt to Viv and Nora; the same for Alice to Marci's two sons. Alice sometimes thought her girls were closer to Marci than to Brooke and Celia.

"They're quite spectacular," Stella said, admiration in her eyes as she turned away from the view of the sculpture garden.

"What was the Inn like when you came to check it out for your wedding?" Alice asked, unable to contain her curiosity any longer. She was dying to have another conversation about Jack and Linda, and this might be her only chance.

Stella settled back into the couch and David put his arm around her shoulders. They both looked lost in memory. "Do you remember the terrible wallpaper?" Stella asked her husband. He nodded, but kept his gaze out toward the shore. "Even though wallpaper was the thing back then, it was just dark and gaudy. I can't believe people ever thought that was the right way to decorate."

"And there was no screened porch. I can't remember the exact layout," David said, "but it was definitely not as welcoming and comfortable as you've made it."

Stella nodded in agreement. "The rooms were downstairs still. I think they were smaller and there were more than four. The main floor was much more broken up. I can't remember where the owners lived."

"Jack and Linda Lewis," Alice interrupted. This was her chance to get more information about them.

"Right. What a lovely couple they were."

"You said she was pregnant when you met them?" Alice prompted.

"Not when we met them. We came in the fall to set our wedding date. But when they had that terrible fire, she was a few months pregnant. I couldn't even tell. We came a week before the fire and she told us. We were meeting with caterers then." Stella sighed. "We ended up with no caterer and I couldn't be happier today. The wedding really doesn't matter. What matters is who you choose."

Alice couldn't agree more. She'd chosen Peter and loved every day she shared with him.

"I love what you've done with the building. The rooms are perfect. And this porch!" Stella gushed.

"Thank you." Alice paused, unsure how to get more information about Jack and Linda without telling them her connection to them. She didn't see any other path than the truth. "I asked about Jack and Linda because I actually just learned about them before your arrival yesterday. They just passed away two months ago in a small plane crash."

Stella's hand flew to her chest. "I didn't know. I hadn't heard their names in fifty years. Honestly, I'm surprised I even remembered them."

"I had never heard their names until yesterday morning. They left me everything they owned."

Stella looked as confused as Alice had felt yesterday at her meeting with Mr. Thompson. David's expression didn't change as he gazed toward the water. Alice couldn't even tell if he was listening.

"But... you'd never heard of them before?" Stella asked,

now much more interested. She leaned forward, nearly sliding right off the couch in her excitement for more.

"They were my birth parents," Alice said, trying out the truth. It had been less than a day since she'd learned that part of her personal history and Stella and David were the first people she'd told. Other than trying to tell Peter in the Great Beyond. "I only knew their first names until a lawyer showed up at my door yesterday with information about their estate."

Stella's eyes didn't waver from Alice. "She was pregnant with you, wasn't she?" she asked. Alice was surprised that Stella put the pieces together so quickly—faster than Alice had yesterday.

Alice nodded.

"They lost everything and didn't think they could care for you," Stella continued. She leaned back into the couch. "My goodness. What a decision. Can you imagine?"

Alice wasn't sure if Stella was asking her or David, so Alice answered. "I've been thinking the same thing. I spent so many years—what feels like a lifetime ago now—wondering about my birth parents. Now I have their names and the reason they gave me away. But I know nothing else about them. Somehow, I feel like I know them, though."

"You have kids?" Stella asked.

Alice nodded, thinking of what she would tell Nora and Viv about Jack and Linda when they came over this afternoon.

"Then you know how hard it must have been for Linda to make that decision. And Jack, too," she added.

Alice kept nodding. "Indeed," was all she managed to say, wondering again what she would have done if she'd faced the same challenges that Jack and Linda had early in her pregnancy. She was thankful she hadn't had to make those same kinds of choices.

"You've had quite the opening, it seems," Stella said, then put her hand on David's knee and leaned forward. She turned to her husband and asked, "Shall we?" Then she turned to Alice to explain. "We're planning a walk through the sculptures this morning, then heading down to the beach to relax."

Alice smiled. Their day sounded like the perfect way to enjoy each other's love and company. "If you need anything, don't hesitate to ask."

Stella and David took their leave from the porch and Alice headed back into the kitchen. She picked up the used dishes on the way and loaded the dishwasher. The newlyweds likely wouldn't be up for some time still, so she let her thoughts about Jack and Linda swim through her mind.

When her family showed up this afternoon, was she going to tell them? She wasn't sure she was ready to share that part of her past yet.

CHAPTER NINETEEN

Celia enjoyed the best night's sleep of the last four months, thanks to having her husband next to her again. For all of her imagining what could have driven him away, never had she considered that it was something she could so easily move past. But she was ready and willing to keep him around.

Mitch's chest rose and fell as he slowly woke up. Rather than watching him—which Celia always thought was creepy—she got out of bed and started the coffee, something Mitch usually did. For four months, she'd been making just enough for herself.

Minutes later, Mitch joined her in the kitchen. "I overslept," he told her, slipping his hands around her waist and kissing her neck.

"I thought so." Celia turned around and hugged the man she loved.

Last night had been blissful. She'd missed Mitch, despite what he'd put her through. It wasn't just the comfort of knowing him for ten years and being married for six that brought her forgiveness so quickly.

It was love.

"Have you thought about tonight?" Celia asked, keeping her hands around his neck.

Mitch leaned back so he could look her in the eye. She wasn't sure what his answer would be, but she desperately wanted him to come to the Inn for dinner with her family.

They were starting again. Picking up where they'd left off. Tonight would be the perfect opportunity to let everyone know, even those who didn't know he'd moved out.

"I have thought about it," he said, his blue eyes never leaving her own. "It'll be tough, but I'll come."

Celia breathed a sigh of relief and kissed him again. "Thank you."

"Thank you for listening yesterday. I can't believe it took me so long to tell you. I'm sorry."

"Enough with the sorries," Celia said. "We're done with that. You're here, and we're moving forward. Now get your coffee and get to work."

Celia didn't want him to leave the condo but she had to get to work, too. Saturdays were busy at the bookstore and she always got there early to make sure everything was ready.

"Before I go, I have something else I wanted to tell you." He paused, and Celia was unsure what might be coming. "Getting to know Dylan has been one of the best parts of my adult life. I was thinking... maybe we *could* have a baby together."

Celia was stunned. The only path she'd ever heard from him was no kids. And she'd accepted that. Her own hesitancies around babies kept her from really pushing parenthood.

"Are you sure?" she asked.

Mitch nodded. "You don't have to answer right now. But I know you'd make a great mom. And I'm starting to think that I'll make an okay dad."

Celia laughed. "You'll be better than okay," she teased. "You'll be great, too. I'll take your offer under consideration."

Mitch leaned forward and wrapped Celia in a hug that she never wanted to end. She could stay there forever and be happy.

"Now, get to work," she said again when he let go of her.

Mitch smiled but did as he was told, filling his travel mug to the brim and grabbing a plain bagel, not even taking time for cream cheese. He was already late. Celia watched him go and then got ready for her bike ride to work.

As she rode, Celia considered the circumstances of Mitch's offer. She couldn't help but wonder if he was feeling guilty about leaving for four months without a word. Well, she knew he was. But was that why he suddenly offered to become a parent with her?

Celia had given up thinking about motherhood so long ago that this change in mindset totally blindsided her. Was she ready anymore to have a baby? Would Dylan be enough? That way she could skip the part of parenthood that really scared her—the newborn and infant stages.

By the time she reached Celia's Bookshelf, Celia didn't have an answer. She stashed her bike in her office and tried to push the idea of pregnancy and babies out of her mind, instead focusing on work.

Celia took a deep breath to leave everything from this morning and the last four months out of her work, and remembered that she and Alice hadn't connected yesterday. She felt even more guilty for not following up with her sister when lunch didn't work out. Celia had been the one to skip the party on Thursday, and now it had been over twenty-four hours that she could have apologized in person. She picked up her phone to make things right and was surprised to see a message from Alice.

Sorry I missed you yesterday. Big day here. Brooke told me about Mitch. Sorry to hear. Let's catch up tonight at the Inn with Mom and Dad.

Sent while Celia had been riding to work.

Celia should have made a bigger effort to see Alice yesterday, but with Mitch's arrival, everything else had been forgotten. Tonight's dinner would be the best she was going to get. She was starting over with Mitch, and this could be a new beginning with Alice. They'd had their own relationship challenges over the years, but that didn't mean those had to continue.

Celia could do better. She *would* do better.

There was only a half hour before Celia opened. Saturdays she opened at 9:30 instead of her usual ten. Cori was in charge of the register and helping customers while Celia read for story hour. The teen walked in the front door and it was time to get to business.

Celia booted up the computer at the register and made sure Cori was all set, then brought the three kids' books she'd be reading to the children's area. They were all new books, published within the last six months, and encouraged gardening and growing. Celia was excited for what she hoped would be plenty of kids going home with new books.

Promptly at ten, Celia sat down with a small group of kids. There were only four families, and Brooke wasn't even there. She was disappointed, but did her best not to let that feeling come through in her reading. For a beautiful June Saturday, Celia knew four families was a success.

After Celia read the first book, the bells on the door jingled and she glanced in the direction to see who her customer was. It was Brooke, with Emma and Noah in tow. She switched gears for a summer song, giving her sister, niece, and nephew a chance to sit down before the next story began.

All the kids seemed to enjoy the books. They flocked to them when Celia placed them on her chair and she stood up after reading and singing. Celia made her way to Brooke, getting caught briefly a couple times by other parents, thanking her for the Saturday morning activity.

"Hey. Sorry we were late," Brooke said, watching Emma rather than making eye contact.

"No problem." Celia knew Brooke rarely made it anywhere on time when the kids were with her. "You staying for a bit?" Checking out the used books was one of Emma and Noah's favorite things after story hour.

Brooke shook her head, still not looking at Celia. "Noah has a soccer game."

"You're coming to dinner tonight, right?"

Brooke nodded. Her kids continued to hold her attention. Celia got the funny feeling that Brooke wasn't telling her something.

"Are you okay?" Celia asked. She desperately wanted to tell her that Mitch had come by yesterday and moved back in with her. They were on the mend and things were looking up.

Brooke nodded again. "Fine."

With that, Celia couldn't hold in her news any longer. "Mitch came back home."

Brooke finally turned away from her kids, now heading toward the used book section of the store, and her jaw dropped. "When?"

"Yesterday afternoon."

"He wasn't staying at Stuart's," Brooke blurted out.

Celia couldn't tell if that was meant to hurt her or not. But it made her heart skip a beat. "You knew?"

Brooke seemed to realize what she'd said and her cheeks flushed. "I just learned it yesterday from Stuart. I went to talk to him about the golf tournament."

Celia nodded, remembering that part of their conversation. "And you didn't tell me?" It wasn't news to Celia that Mitch hadn't been staying with Stuart, but Brooke could have let her know, nonetheless.

"I didn't mean to not tell you," Brooke said, still not acting like herself. Something wasn't right but Celia couldn't tell what. "I'm sorry that I didn't. Is everything okay with you and Mitch now?"

"We're working it out." Celia was about to launch into the news about Dylan and why Mitch hadn't been staying with Stuart, but Brooke spoke first.

"I'm glad. Hey, I've gotta get the kids and get moving. I'll see you tonight, right?"

Brooke was already walking away as Celia nodded dumbly after her. "Yeah, okay," she said to Brooke's back.

Celia caught up with another family she saw every Saturday, happy to see that the daughter was pestering her mother for a new book. As she said goodbye, she saw Brooke leave with Emma and Noah protesting. She sent her niece and nephew a wave but neither of them saw it.

When the families with young kids had made their purchases and left, Celia had a quiet moment where she could consider what might be going on with Brooke or if she was overthinking the whole interaction.

Yesterday, Brooke was worried about losing the contract

with the country club. Maybe that wasn't worked out yet; Brooke hadn't said.

But the way she delivered the news about Mitch not staying at Stuart's wasn't like Brooke. She was usually more considerate. She was definitely distracted, that was for sure.

But why, Celia didn't know.

CHAPTER TWENTY

Brooke shuffled the kids into the car, knowing she could have stayed longer. They still had plenty of time to drive home, get lunches packed, and get Noah ready for his soccer game. She just couldn't be around Celia right now. Not with a baby growing inside her womb and still stressed out about that reality.

She'd have to get over it by tonight's dinner with her whole family.

Brooke knew that part of her guilt over the whole interaction at the bookstore was that she'd already been blessed with three wonderful kids, a fourth now on its way, while Celia had been devastated when Mitch told her he didn't want kids. That conversation had taken years to settle, but Brooke knew that a part of Celia would always wonder *what if*.

The what ifs were a dangerous path.

Telling Celia that she was pregnant while she was trying to save her marriage felt like slapping her little sister in the face. She wouldn't do that to her.

Back at home, Brooke lay down for a few minutes while

Jared took charge. He packed the lunches and made sure Noah had everything he needed for his soccer game. He even pulled Tina away from her allotted one hour of weekend screen time without an argument. Brooke had no idea how he kept his cool against her whine and eye rolls.

Then she was back into the car, wishing she could take a real nap, but thankful she at least didn't have to drive.

"How are you feeling?" Jared asked when they sat down in the shade near the soccer field for lunch. Noah would be starving after his soccer game, but that didn't mean the girls had to wait to eat.

Brooke shrugged. She didn't feel like she was going to lose her breakfast like yesterday, but she certainly didn't feel like herself.

"What's wrong, Mom?" Tina asked unexpectedly. "You're not eating. You didn't even eat dinner last night."

They had gotten pizza, after all, but Brooke had barely taken a bite. She didn't think anyone but Jared had noticed.

She was wrong.

Brooke looked to her husband, wanting to tell Tina the truth. Jared knew how she felt; they'd talked about it more last night in bed. He gave the slightest nod, agreeing that Brooke could tell them about the baby. She wished Noah was there for the news, but they could tell him after his game.

"Well..." Now that the moment was here, she wasn't sure how to start. "You guys are going to have another little sister or brother. I'm pregnant," she said. Tina knew enough about reproduction to know what that meant. Emma, not so much. Brooke braced herself for the questions.

"Why?" Tina asked, confusion written across her face. "I thought you and Dad said three kids was enough."

That was not the reaction Brooke had expected from

her oldest daughter. She looked to Jared and they both laughed. "You're not wrong, honey. Three kids are enough. But four will be enough, too."

She wasn't about to tell her kids that she and Jared hadn't *meant* to have another baby.

"Where is it?" Emma asked. "Can we get it after soccer?"

Here it was, the many questions Brooke had expected. "In my tummy," Brooke said.

"Mom, the baby's not in your tummy," Tina protested. "It's in your uterus. You always tell me to use the right words, so you should, too."

Brooke nodded. "You're right, the baby is in my uterus, below my tummy," she explained to Emma, not sure she wanted to go down this road anymore, especially in public. They were set away from the soccer field while the team warmed up, but there were plenty of other families around that could possibly overhear where this conversation was headed.

"How did it get there? Did you eat it?" Emma asked.

Brooke couldn't help it this time. She laughed. "No, sweetie. I didn't eat it. It's growing inside my body and then when it's big enough, it'll come out and we'll have another baby."

"How does it get out?" Emma asked. "Is it going to crawl out your mouth?"

"Through her vagina," Tina said, her teacher voice in place.

"She must have a big vagina if a baby can fit through it."

Emma's face was dead serious, but even Jared laughed this time.

The laughter didn't deter Emma from asking more

questions. "When will it be big enough? Next week?" she asked.

"Not until February," Brooke said, knowing that would mean nothing to her four-year-old.

"Is that before Christmas? Can we give the baby a Christmas present? We'll have to tell Santa about it so he doesn't forget to bring it presents?"

"February is after Christmas," Tina helpfully explained.

Brooke braced herself for whatever might come next, but there was a long stretch where the girls and Jared ate in quiet. Finally, Emma asked Brooke, "Are you not eating lunch because the baby's not hungry?"

Brooke smiled. "No, I'm not eating because I'm not hungry. I'll make sure to feed the baby whenever it's hungry."

"How will you know it's hungry? Will it cry? Josie, at school, has a new baby and she said it's always crying."

"No. I'll get hungry when the baby is hungry. Then I'll eat and the baby will eat whatever I eat," Brooke explained.

"How do you feed it?"

Tina jumped in before Brooke could answer. "There's a rope that keeps the baby connected to Mom. Food and blood go through it from Mom to the baby."

It took everything Brooke had not to burst into laughter at Tina's understanding of the umbilical cord. She caught Jared's eye and saw that his face was turning red from not laughing.

"Is it a girl or a boy?" Emma asked.

"We don't know yet. We haven't seen it." Brooke was glad this was an easier one to answer.

"If it's a girl, can we name it Julia?"

Brooke had no idea where that name came from. There

was no Julia she'd ever heard of at school, nor in a book they'd read, or show they'd watched. "Umm... maybe."

"If it's a boy, will it have a penis like Noah?"

"Of course it will," Tina answered. "Every boy has a penis."

Brooke decided Jared might have been right. Maybe they should have waited to tell the kids. But it was too late now. They were going down this road, at a soccer game, no less.

"Why don't I bring Emma and Tina to the playground," Jared suggested. "You can sit and watch the game."

Brooke was relieved. She didn't want other parents overhearing Emma's questions before her own family knew about the baby.

"Great," Brooke agreed.

"Go ahead. It looks like they're starting. Noah likes having you there. I'll clean this up when we're done."

Brooke kissed her daughters and husband, then brought her folding chair to the edge of the soccer field. She could see both the game and the playground from the sidelines and gave Noah a quick wave just before the referee blew the starting whistle.

There was an hour ahead of Brooke where she could think about how to break this news to the rest of her family. She knew her parents would be overjoyed, along with Alice.

But there was still Celia. She didn't know how Celia would react.

CHAPTER TWENTY-ONE

"What are they like?" Nora asked Alice as they enjoyed iced tea on the screened porch in the middle of the afternoon. Astrid and Karl were once again basking in the sun—and each other's love—down at the Inn's beach.

"Young and in love," Alice told her daughter. Nora was not much younger than the newlywed guests. In another life, they might have been friends. "It's nice to have company here."

"Viv and I can come stay when you don't have guests."

"I'd love that. You know you're always welcome." Alice would love nothing more than for her daughters to enjoy time at the Inn with her.

"Where is everyone hiding?" Viv's voice came through the Inn and Alice stood to find her. Viv beat her to it.

"I didn't expect you until closer to dinner," Alice said, wrapping Viv in a hug. "I'll get another glass." Viv tried to protest, but Alice left her daughters on the porch, anyway.

Now that both girls were here, Alice wanted to tell them about Jack and Linda Lewis. They had a right to know about their biological grandparents, even if they'd never meet them. Besides the glass for Viv, Alice sliced some more of Heather's blueberry bread and brought everything back to the porch.

"What's this?" Nora asked. She had an epic sweet tooth that had somehow not led to many cavities in childhood.

Alice set the plate on the table and the glass in front of Viv. "I didn't make it."

Nora rolled her eyes. "You don't have to open with that, Mom."

"You're right. It's blueberry bread. From yesterday's farmer's market." Alice sat back down, anticipation building in how her girls would take her news.

Viv and Nora both took slices of the bread, Viv taking only half while Nora searched for the biggest piece. Alice sat back, not hungry.

"How's your first weekend going, Mom?" Viv asked between bites.

"Great. Newlyweds are down by the beach," Alice pointed toward the couple by the water, "and an older couple celebrating their fiftieth anniversary."

For the first time, Alice realized she'd never be able to reach that milestone with Peter. Or anyone else, for that matter. It made her heart hurt, but only for a moment. She was consciously practicing being thankful for what she did get to share with him, not wishing for what she wouldn't have.

"No issues?" Viv asked.

Alice shook her head. "Just a forgotten charging cord, but I had the right one, thanks to you, Viv. That was smart to keep everything—and organized."

Viv shrugged. "No biggie."

"I have had quite the weekend, though. Nothing with

the guests," she added quickly when Nora's and Viv's faces both fell. "And not bad. Interesting, but not bad."

Alice paused, considering what to start with—that she'd learned who her birth parents were or that they had passed away before she ever got the chance to meet them and left her everything they had.

"A lawyer came by Friday morning with... news. You remember me telling you both that I never found my birth parents?" Both girls nodded, looks of expectation changing their faces from the earlier concern. "Well, he was representing their estate at the time of their deaths. They left everything to me."

Alice wasn't sure what she expected, but stunned silence shouldn't have been a surprise. When her daughters finally regained their voices, the questions came fast.

Alice explained as best she could what she knew—that Jack and Linda Lewis had once owned this inn but had lost everything during Linda's pregnancy with Alice and they made the choice to give her up for adoption; that they died in a small plane crash two months ago and they bequeathed their entire estate to Alice. There really wasn't a lot of information.

"Are you going to their house?" Nora asked.

Alice shook her head. "I'm respecting the privacy that they lived with and will use a company to clean it out, then a realtor to stage it and sell it." Alice still had to let Mr. Thompson know what she'd decided. There had been a moment when she'd considered going so she could learn about her birth parents, but then chose to respect their privacy. She no longer felt a right to dive into their personal effects.

"How much was there?" Viv asked. "Sorry, can I ask that? I'm just curious."

"There was plenty," Alice said. "I'm thankful, too, since I spent everything from your dad on the Inn. It takes some pressure off to turn a profit overnight. I'll be okay."

"If they lost everything in the fire fifty years ago and had to start over, where did their money come from?" Viv asked.

Alice shook her head. "I don't know. Their lawyer wouldn't tell me anything that wasn't in his folders. And I'm not sure I want to dig into their lives. If I'm supposed to know, the information will come to me."

Alice watched her daughters exchange a look. They seemed to have a secret language where they could have a whole conversation with just their eyes. That always amazed Alice.

"You're more patient and accepting than I am," Nora admitted. Alice knew that was true.

She smiled at her girls. "At my age, you realize what matters. And what happened in the past is far less important than what's in front of me. I'd rather live knowing that Jack and Linda cared enough to give me to a loving family than find out some other hidden truth."

Footsteps in the Inn made all three women turn away from the untouched iced tea and nearly empty plate of blueberry bread. Alice saw her parents walking through the sitting room and her heart leaped. Despite the challenging relationship she sometimes had with her mother, she was happy to see them.

Viv and Nora jumped out of their seats in their rush to envelop their grandparents in hugs.

WITH THE SUN sinking to the west, Alice's sisters and their families finally arrived. The biggest surprise was not that Brooke was on time, but that Celia was not alone. Alice had not expected Mitch to be with her.

They brought chairs out to the west lawn to enjoy the sun, the warm June evening, and the newly uncovered statues together.

"So, Celia," Alice said once everyone was together. "It seems you have something to share with us."

The animosity Alice had felt toward Celia since Wednesday night's surprise arrival and Thursday night's no-show disappeared with her presence tonight. She could see that her youngest sister was happier than she'd been in months with Mitch back by her side.

"Mitch moved back in yesterday," Celia said, the joy dripping from her words and her smile. She turned to her husband and Alice saw love in their eyes. The same love that she and Peter shared for a quarter century.

"Congratulations," Alice said, giving Celia a hug. Then she turned to Mitch and, in the most severe voice she could muster, said, "If you ever leave my little sister like that again, I'll come after you."

Celia and Brooke burst into hysterics, knowing that the worst Alice could do was kill a mosquito. Mitch seemed to take her seriously, though.

"Don't worry. I have no intention of making that mistake twice."

Conversation bubbled around them, everyone catching up with Alice's parents. Their grandkids couldn't get enough of their Grandma and Grandpa, who couldn't get a moment's peace. But Alice could see that they were enjoying every minute of it.

With no break in sight, Alice knew that she would have to take it upon herself to let everyone know that she had finally located—or that she had been located by—her birth parents. The only person Alice worried about taking the news poorly was her mother.

Alice held up her glass and gently banged it with her wedding band. Everyone turned in her direction and Alice almost chickened out. Was this how she wanted to tell everyone about Jack and Linda?

There was no turning back. Everyone looked to her expectantly.

"It's so nice to have everyone here," Alice started. "And while I have your attention, I wanted to tell everyone some exciting news."

"This Inn is turning a profit," Brooke guessed.

Alice laughed. "That'd be something," Alice agreed. "But no."

She paused for a moment and caught Viv's eye. Her older daughter nodded at her. Alice hadn't told her girls that she was going to share this news tonight, but Viv seemed to know.

"I was contacted by Jack and Linda Lewis, the people who gave me life." Alice looked to her mother before she continued. "They may have *given* me life, but everyone here has *been* my life. Jack and Linda died two months ago and left me their estate."

Alice was once again met with stunned silence, just like her daughters' reactions this afternoon.

"So, that's it," she said, trying to lighten the mood. "Just thought everyone should know."

Alice's mom made a move toward her but Celia interrupted. "While we're sharing news," she started, then turned to Mitch, who smiled his encouragement. "Mitch learned he has a twelve-year-old son named Dylan. And we decided to try to have a baby of our own."

If Alice had been surprised by her news, this was truly

conversation-stopping—had there been any conversation going.

Brooke was the first one to break the silence. "I guess now's as good a time as any to tell everyone that we're having another baby."

All eyes traveled from one sister to the next—Alice to Celia to Brooke. This was not the reunion with her parents that she'd expected.

"Wait—Jack and Linda Lewis are your birth parents?" Jared finally said. "From southern Vermont?" he added.

Alice nodded.

"They created a series of kids' books about adoption. They worked with high-profile advocates and policy makers and psychologists. They ended up with a huge contract from Netflix and managed to talk their way into a onetime lump sum payment instead of royalties. Which ended up being very lucrative since the show never made it past the pilot," Jared explained.

Alice now understood where their money had come from. While they hadn't left her millions, they'd certainly recovered from the loss of their inn fifty years ago.

"It sounds like we have plenty to celebrate," Alice's mom said. "Any Champagne around?"

"In the fridge!" Alice announced, excited that everyone had something to celebrate tonight. "Leftover from Thursday's launch party, thanks to Brooke."

"I'll help you get it," Brooke said, joining Alice on her way back inside.

As they walked away from the rest of their family, Alice asked, "How are you feeling? And congratulations. I think?"

Brooke rolled her eyes and groaned. "It wasn't planned, I can assure you of that. But we're rolling with it. You remember how awful I felt with Emma? This one seems even worse. But right now, I'm okay. I was worried how Celia would take the news that we were having a fourth kid when I know she had tried to get Mitch to go down the parenthood path in the past. I'm excited for them."

Alice agreed. "Hey, did anyone bring dinner? I think Mom told me the other day we were getting Thai food."

Brooke laughed. "I don't think anyone placed an order."

They brought out two bottles of Champagne and filled everyone's glasses, then Alice asked about dinner.

"I thought Mom was ordering it," Celia said, looking toward her parents.

"We spent all day driving. I thought Brooke was ordering it since she's the best at organizing parties," Alice's mother said, looking to Brooke.

"I don't think anyone ever asked me to get it," Brooke clarified. "But I'm happy to place an order now."

"That'd be great," Alice agreed. "I'm starving."

Brooke left and Alice sidled up to her girls, who were standing together at the base of the nearest sculpture. "I'm proud of you, Mom," Viv said, placing one arm around Alice's shoulder.

"Me too," Nora agreed. "I don't know how you turned Dad's death around into something happy so quickly."

Alice knew she couldn't have done it without the never-ending support of her family. "Nothing to it but to do it," Alice said, smiling. That had been one of Peter's go-to phrases to get their girls moving. It hardly ever worked, but he'd never stopped trying.

Alice put an arm around each of her daughters, pulling them close. As long as they were near, she had everything she needed.

"I heard something about you and Aiden being a thing?" Alice said, not looking at Viv.

"Hope told you, didn't she?" Viv asked. Alice could hear a smile in her voice. "I knew it wouldn't stay secret for long."

"Why were you keeping secrets from Mom?" Nora teased.

"I wasn't. It just wasn't serious so I didn't exactly tell the world. But it's over now. Nothing happened," she quickly assured Alice. "Just didn't feel quite right. We have plenty of the same friends and I don't think that'll change."

Alice was happy to have everyone close. She, of course, wished Peter was here to share in her joy and the milestones that everyone seemed to be reaching at the same time, but the past couldn't be changed. Alice hugged each of her daughters, and then the three of them returned to the rest of their family for a feast.

I hope you enjoyed THE NORTH STAR INN. Join Alice, Marci, and Lila on their journeys into their futures in the next book in the series, THE ANNIVERSARY EFFECT.

ABOUT THE AUTHOR

Stacey Rae lives in Vermont where she can be found building fairy houses, sword fighting dragons, and searching for wizard magic with her two young children.

Made in the USA
Coppell, TX
26 May 2021